Cracked Classics

Crack open all the books in

Cracked Classics

#1: Trapped in Transylvania
(Dracula)

#2: Mississippi River Blues
(The Adventures of Tom Sawyer)

#3: What a Trip!
(Around the World in Eighty Days)

#4: Humbug Holiday
(A Christmas Carol)

Coming soon!
#5: X Marks the Spot
(Treasure Island)

A Christmas Carol

Humbug Holiday

By Tony Abbott

Hyperion
New York

Text copyright © 2002 by Tony Abbott
Cracked Classics, Volo, and the Volo colophon are trademarks of Disney Enterprises, Inc.

Printed in the United States of America
First Edition
1 3 5 7 9 10 8 6 4 2
This book is set in 11.5-pt. Cheltenham.

ISBN 0-7868-1327-X
Visit www.volobooks.com

Chapter 1

"Hilli-ho, Devin!" a voice called out as I crashed through the front doors of Palmdale Middle School and tramped into the cafeteria.

"Yo-ho, there, Frankie!" the voice chirped as my best-friend-forever-despite-the-fact-that-she's-a-girl Frankie Lang breezed into the caf alongside me.

Frankie and I screeched to a stop.

The chirpy voice belonged to Mr. Wexler, our English teacher. He came trotting toward us now, a huge grin on his face and his wispy hair flying up behind him.

"Warning, warning," I said. "Mr. Wexler smiling. We have suddenly entered an alternate dimension of weirdness!"

Frankie chuckled. "Or maybe it's just good old Christmas spirit. After all, it's only two days till the big day."

"Which translates to—the last day of school before vacation!" I added.

"Well, well!" Mr. Wexler said, his face still beaming. "What do you think? Pretty wonderful, isn't it?"

He waved his arm around the cafeteria as if he were swishing an invisible cape.

The place was jammed with kids from our English class, taping red and green streamers to the ceiling, stringing twinkly white lights around the fake-frosted windows, decorating a Christmas tree, and piling up holiday baked goods on a couple of long tables.

"All this, just for us?" I said. "I feel honored. . . ."

Mr. Wexler laughed. "Ha! Good one, Devin. Now, really. What have you two brought in today, hmm?"

"Just ourselves, for a great day at school!" Frankie said, her smile twinkling like those Christmas lights.

"A great *last* day of school," I said, just because it sounded so good.

But as cheery as Frankie and I were getting, our teacher wasn't. He pointed up to a huge banner hanging over our heads. It read:

6TH-GRADE COMMUNITY CHRISTMAS BANQUET
FOOD DONATIONS DUE—TODAY!

"You do know our Christmas Banquet is today, don't you?" he asked. "We're hosting the Palmdale Homeless Shelter. You were supposed to bring in food for the charity dinner. You knew about this."

I blinked at the guy. "Are you sure we knew about this? Because my brain tells me we sort of didn't."

"You should have known about it," he replied. "We've talked about it for the last month in class—"

"Oh, in class!" said Frankie. Then she turned to me and whispered. "There's the problem, Devin. You were probably snoring too loud for me to hear."

I grumbled at my friend. "I don't snore. I sleep quite soundly, thank you—"

"We've talked about how there are families, even in sunny Palmdale, who don't eat as well as we do," Mr. Wexler went on. "Some people—children like yourselves—don't have as many clothes as we do."

"That's not good," I said.

"Hundreds of people in our own town don't have proper food or shelter," our teacher said. "Our Christmas Banquet is just one way to help. It's part of the book project we're working on. Remember?"

Frankie frowned. "I guess we forgot to remember."

"Or maybe we remembered to forget," I said.

A huge sigh came from our teacher. "So, you didn't bring in food. Did you at least read the book?"

We stared at our teacher.

3

One thing you have to realize about Frankie and me is that as bad as we are about remembering (or even hearing) about school stuff, we're probably worse at the whole reading thing.

People say we don't read well because we fail to grasp that we're actually supposed to open the books, not just carry them around.

I say it's because they cram too many words in books and make you read all of the words, or it doesn't count.

"Do you even *have* the book?" Mr. Wexler asked, setting his hands on his hips in that out-of-patience way he has. "You both have backpacks. Are they empty?"

"Of course not!" Frankie scoffed. She tipped her backpack over. A hairbrush fell out. "Now it's empty."

Mr. Wexler grumbled, then turned to me. "Devin?"

"Mine's not empty, but it sure isn't crammed with books!" I said.

Narrowing his eyes, Mr. Wexler stepped over to a table, picked up a thin book, and held it up in front of us. "It's called *A Christmas Carol*. Jog any memories?"

"Wait a second," I said. "I know this book. Isn't it all about a girl named Carol who wears red and green at the same time?"

"That's right," said Frankie. "Even though red and green together is a way tremendous fashion risk. I

4

heard about that book, too. Wasn't there a movie—"

"Not even close," Mr. Wexler cut in, wrinkling his eyebrows. Or, I should say eye*brow*, since he really only has one. It stretches over both eyes, is very bushy, and wiggles like a fuzzy black caterpillar when he gets mad.

It was wiggling now.

He shook his head at me. "Frankly, I expected much better things. . . ."

"No, I'm Devin. She's Frankly," I said.

I was joking. But actually we both knew why Mr. Wexler expected better things from us. You see, even though we find it tough to read, Frankie and I have actually gotten good grades in Mr. Wexler's English class.

How, you ask?

I'll tell you, I say!

In a single word—the zapper gates.

That's three words, Frankie would say, because she's such a math whiz.

What are the zapper gates, you ask?

I will tell you that, too.

The zapper gates are these old, supposedly busted security gates that our school librarian, Mrs. Figglehopper, keeps in the library workroom. But—as Frankie and I have found out—those gates are anything but busted.

5

They are the most amazing—and secret—things ever. What happens when you get near them is—

Wait, I'll tell you later. Mr. Wexler is talking again.

"Perhaps you'd both better just report to the library," he said. "I'm sure Mrs. Figglehopper will find a copy of the book for you to read!"

"But if we go to the library, we'll miss the beginning of the banquet," I protested.

"And while you're there," he continued, "maybe you can think about how important this event is to everyone—and why it should be important to you, too."

"But, Mr. Wexler, there's food here. And we love food," Frankie pleaded. "Do we have to go right now?"

He gave us the eyebrow.

We went right then.

Chapter 2

"This is so not fair," I grumbled.

Frankie snorted. "Except that it probably is. We totally blew it, Devin. We're slackers. Get used to it."

"Oh, I'm used to it," I said. "It's other people who keep wanting to change us. As if that's possible!"

We trudged out of the caf and entered the crazy maze of hallways to the library. Actually, the library was practically next door to the cafeteria.

It's just that Frankie and I always take the long way.

Because, for us, the library usually spells work. Plus a few other words, like danger and weirdness and trouble and—did I mention work?

As we slunk past the main office for the fifth time

and up to the double doors of the library, Frankie stopped.

"What's that?" she asked, leaning *very* close to me.

"Um, I think it's called my personal space—"

"No, that smell."

"What smell? I don't smell anything. There's no smell. Say, isn't the weather mild today—"

She gasped. "It's chocolate!"

"No, it's not. Chocolate? Here? That's just nutty! Have you been chewing your pencils again—"

"You have chocolate!" she said, grabbing me by the shoulders. "Your mother made her famous chocolate-chip cookies, didn't she? Oh! She did! I can smell them in your backpack! Open!"

"No way! If there are chocolate-chip cookies in my bag, then by law they're mine!" I jerked my pack away.

But she turned that look on me. The one where she tries to bore a hole through my brain just by using her eyes. Very effective. I started feeling dizzy right away.

"Okay, obeying . . ." I mumbled.

Carefully, I lifted the flap on my pack, loosened the drawstring, and pulled open the top. The aroma of chocolate-chip cookies blossomed out into the hallway.

"Oh, man!" she murmured, her eyes getting huge.

"Oh, man, is right," I said. "Four dozen silver-dollar-size special Christmas chocolate-chip cookies totally home-baked. Mom must have put them in my backpack for a lunchtime surprise. Isn't she the best?"

Frankie took one look at my beaming face, then burst into a short, sudden laugh. "Devin, you walnut! Those cookies aren't for your lunch! Your mother sent them in for the Christmas Banquet soup-kitchen thingy—"

"That's crazy talk!" I blurted out. "Cookies don't go with soup!"

"Devin, trust me. Why would your mom *ever* give you forty-eight cookies for lunch?"

I thought about it. "Because it's Christmas?"

"Christmas Banquet, you mean."

I stomped my foot. "Oh, man. I can't believe it! And I thought it was just a case of awesome holiday spirit. I should have known it was too good to be true!"

"You'd better tell Mr. Wexler that you brought food."

"Oh, no," I said, waving my arms. "It's too late for that. My stomach already got a whiff of these cookies. If I don't feed it, it'll rebel. I'll give cookies next time—"

"Devin, what if there is no next time? What if this is the last Christmas Banquet ever? What if those people go hungry? What if you never get a second chance?"

"Now you're scaring me, Frankie," I said. "Besides, I'm pretty sure the cookies will get stale just sitting out on some table waiting for people. And staleness is a major health risk. They'll stay fresher in my backpack."

She squinted at me. "It couldn't be that you're just being stingy and want to eat them all yourself?"

I shook my head. "I'm only thinking of the cookies!"

"I know you are. That's the problem." Then she took a whiff. "They do smell good."

"I'm sure they are good," I said.

"You have enough in there to feed an army."

"Yeah, an army of one."

Frankie frowned. "Give me one—"

"Kkkkk!" I said. "What did you say? *Keee-oooo-kkkkk!* Sorry, Frank—*kkk*—kie! Bad—connection! Too much—*kkkk!*—static—"

"Ahem!" boomed a voice over our shoulders.

Whirling around, we saw a woman hustling up behind us. It was Mrs. Figglehopper. The librarian.

Mrs. Figglehopper is a bit older than my mom and a bit younger than my grandmother. She always wears dresses with big flowers on them and her hair tied up in a tight bun. For years, she's been head of books at Palmdale Middle. She is absolutely nutzoid about books.

"And what brings my two favorite students to the library today?" she asked as she opened the double doors and whisked us into her book-filled lair. "Could it be that you haven't really been paying attention in class?"

"That's just a nasty rumor," said Frankie. "But, yeah."

"Actually, we're here to pick up a copy of some book," I told her.

Mrs. Figglehopper stood there with a half-smiling, half-quizzical expression on her face. It was an expression she seemed to use a lot when Frankie and I were around. "Let me guess. Is it called *A Christmas Carol*?"

"How did you know?" asked Frankie.

"Just a hunch," said the librarian. "It's Mr. Wexler's project for the Christmas Banquet. I've given copies to all your classmates, and now I have only one copy left. It's in the workroom. Follow me!"

The workroom was a small room located in the front corner of the library. Inside were tables, a computer, and lots and lots of bookshelves filled with crusty old books.

The zapper gates were also in there, tucked against the back wall. I glanced at them quickly, but

Mrs. Figglehopper stood in the way, holding out a copy of a thin red book. On the cover was a design of gold holly leaves and gold lettering.

"This is my last copy of *A Christmas Carol*. You must be very careful with it. It's quite old. By the way, do you know what it's about?"

"We know what it's not about," I said. "Which is a start."

Mrs. Figglehopper chuckled to herself. "Yes, well, ever since I was old enough to read, I have loved this book," she said. "It was written in 1843 by the famous English novelist Charles Dickens. It's about an old miser named Ebenezer Scrooge."

"Funny name," said Frankie.

"Dickens was famous for his funny names," said Mrs. Figglehopper. "Scrooge is very rich, but very stingy. His heart is cold. He won't use his money for good. He only wants to keep it. But money isn't good if it doesn't help anyone. Money is like . . . like . . ."

"Cookies?" said Frankie, casting a look my way.

"Exactly!" said the librarian. "If you keep cookies too long they'll get moldy and be no good for anyone. And it's the same with Scrooge. He doesn't share. He loves no one, helps no one, has no friends. He doesn't celebrate Christmas a single bit."

"Sounds like a bad sort of man," said Frankie.

"So what happens to this Scrooge guy?" I asked.

12

"Well, he is visited by—"

Brrrnng! The phone rang. "Hold on."

She picked it up, nodded once, said "Good," then hung up and turned back to us. "Mr. Wexler needs me in the cafeteria. The turkeys have just come out of the ovens and I'm going to help carve them. In the meantime, this little red book has some loose pages in the front. Perhaps you could repair them for me before you take it. The glue is in the back of the work-room."

"We'll be late for the Christmas Banquet," I started to say, but Mrs. Figglehopper had already whooshed her way out the doors, heading for the cafeteria.

"Oh, sure," I said. "While everybody's noshing on turkey and stuffing, we're stuck here repairing books."

"It's just a few pages," said Frankie. "We should be able to fix them in a jiffy and get back before the party starts. I'll set up the book, you get the special glue."

"I will get the special glue," I said, giving Frankie the eye, "but I'll take my backpack with me."

While Frankie opened the book to find the loose pages, I poked around for the glue. Of course, the search for glue led me near those crazy old zapper gates.

13

I tried not to stare at them, but I couldn't help myself.

After all, they were the reason we had gotten good grades in English, even though reading was hard for us.

"The zapper gates," I whispered.

Frankie looked up. "Just find the glue, Devin."

The glue. Uh-huh, sure. But listen.

Ordinary library security gates are supposed to go all *zzzt-zzzt* when a book isn't checked out the right way. It was too bad—so Mrs. Figglehopper said—that these particular gates were busted beyond repair.

Uh-uh. No way. Wrong-o!

Frankie and I found out the hard way that these gates *do* work. Only not in any normal regular every-day way. No, no. If a book happens to go through *these* gates, a weird blue blinding bright light flashes out.

Sound impossible?

Of course, it's impossible! And even more impossible is what happens next. The wall behind the gates cracks open—that's right—it cracks open, and the book gets sucked right through the crack! And suddenly you find yourself getting sucked right through after it!

Believe it!

It's happened to Frankie and me a couple of times.

14

And each time it happens, we get all tumbled and rumbled and wumbled around and finally get thrown out smack dab in the first chapter of the book.

That's right. Frankie and me—in the book!

It's crazy. It's impossible. It's ultraweird.

But it happens.

So far, we've been lucky enough to make it back out again. But we've had to read our way to the last page every time. That's why we know the books so well and how we get good grades.

Anyway, I found the glue and went back to the table, pulling up a chair. "Move over a bit," I said. "I want to see the book."

Frankie pulled the book away, with a sudden sly look in her eye that I didn't like. "I'll share the book if you share your cookies."

"Ha, I don't think so!" I said.

"Then, I don't think you can see the book," she said.

"But it's not the same," I protested. "If you share the book with me, the book is still there. But if I share my cookies with you, those cookies are gone."

Frankie frowned. "They belong to the Christmas Banquet, anyway. They're for other people to eat."

"Other people like you?" I said. "I don't think so."

"I only want one."

"Then show me the book."

"Not without a cookie!"

"Not without the book!"

I made a grab for the book. She tried to seize my pack. Our arms got tangled. Our hands collided. And the next thing we knew the book was flying up in the air.

"Get it!" Frankie screamed.

We both jumped for the book. Too late.

The book fell right between the zapper gates.

Zzzzz—kkkkk—zzzzzt! The room flashed with a sudden bright blue light that practically charred my eyeballs. We were thrown to the floor. Then everything quaked and the back wall cracked open and it sucked us through the gates and we tumbled and rolled and fell and bounced down, down, down, and finally out onto a dirty, dark street on a dirty, dark night.

Thick yellow fog rolled over us.

Frankie sat up next to me. We looked at each other.

"Um, sorry about the tussle for the cookies," she said.

"Me, too, for the book," I said.

We looked around at where we were.

"Do you want to say it, or should I?" she asked.

I groaned. "In the spirit of sharing, I have to say it's probably your turn. Go ahead."

Frankie drew in a sharp breath, then said it.

"We're in a book—again!"

16

Chapter 3

I stood up and peered through the fog.

The blue light had faded and the zapper gates were gone. So was the crack in the wall we'd come through.

"Well, so far, so weird," I grumbled. "We're totally in the book now. I hope it's a good one."

Frankie scooped the thin red book up from the street. "And I hope it's not too dark to read."

It nearly was.

The street we were in was narrow, but the fog was so thick that we barely saw the buildings on the other side.

"Okay, we're in some city, probably at night," I said. "An old city, with lots of old stone buildings. We're definitely not in Palmdale anymore."

"Not likely," she said, flipping open to the title page. "It says here the book was published in London. That's in England."

"The birthplace of English class," I mumbled. "It's not present day, either. They have old-fashioned streetlights, which means they don't light up much at all. All in all, it's sort of a cold, gloomy place to put a Christmas story. I mean, hey. Where are the reindeer and snowmen and elves and presents for me?"

In the distance, a clock was sounding out the hour.

Bong! Bong! Bong!

"Three o'clock? Is that right?" wondered Frankie. "It's so dark."

"Dark or not, three o'clock definitely makes it snack time!" I said, reaching around to my backpack.

But even as I did, a hand—a pale, white, very thin hand—darted out of the fog, grabbed my backpack right off my shoulder, and snatched it away.

"Hey, you!" I yelled. "Lay off the chocolaty goodness of my cookies! Give that back—"

But even as I tried to wrestle my pack free of the strange white hand—*whoosh!*—an icy wind swept around me and the hand was gone, and with it—*fwit!*—my entire backpack!

I freaked out. "Frankie, it's gone! Someone stole my backpack! I saw a hand! My cookies are in there!

Who would steal cookies from a kid? Especially a kid who's me? And especially at snack time—"

The fog closed around us, leaving no trace of the thief.

"Maybe the book tells us!" said Frankie "Keep looking while I read!"

I scrambled up and down the cobblestone street, but it was so dark and the fog so thick I couldn't see anything. I had to face it. Whoever took my backpack had escaped.

I straggled back to Frankie. "Nope, he's gone. Weird creepy hand. I didn't even see the rest of him."

"If it even *was* a him," she said.

"Right. Huh? What do you mean?"

Frankie was standing under a street lamp whose yellowy light cast a dull glow onto the book's pages. "Devin, look at this. The actual title of the book is, *A Christmas Carol in Prose, Being a Ghost Story of Christmas.*"

"A g-g-ghost story?" I said. "Are you saying that hand was . . . a . . . *ghost* hand? Mrs. Figglehopper and Mr. Wexler never said anything about ghosts."

"This story says something about ghosts," said Frankie, looking up. "Devin, we're in an actual ghost story."

I shivered. "I didn't sign on for ghosts. A Christmas story, maybe, but no ghosts. I'm not a fan of ghosts. Ghosts haunt people. Which means they'll probably want to haunt me. No, no, this is crazy. Who mixes ghosts and Christmas anyway?"

"Charles Dickens does. He's the guy who wrote it. Good thing it's a skinny book. Maybe your backpack won't be too hard to find."

I wasn't so sure. Even a short book in this time and place didn't seem all that inviting. The weather, for instance, was going to be a problem for California kids like us. It was cold, bleak, and biting everywhere we turned. We could hear people on the other side of the street go wheezing up and down the sidewalk, beating their hands together and stamping their feet on the pavement to keep warm.

"I don't like this," I said, shivering. "Let's read until we get to a good part. Preferably, the part where we find my pack, snarf down my cookies, jump through the zapper gates, and get back to Palmdale in time for a normal, ghost-free Christmas. You read first."

Frankie snorted a snort at me. "Good luck. The fog is too thick to make out the words. And you know what happens when we skip ahead."

I nodded. I knew.

It's one of the major rules of being in a book. If you try to cheat and skip ahead—even a few pages— everything goes kablooey. A big rip appears in the sky over your head and a huge lightning storm starts and you get tossed around until you crash-land in another part of the story. It's not something you want to mess with.

"Okay," I said. "So if we can't read, where do we go? And don't tell me we go ghost hunting—"

Frankie chuckled suddenly. "We go right there!"

I peered through the darkness at what she was pointing at. Hanging not far away was a small sign.

On it were the words SCROOGE AND MARLEY.

"Ebenezer Scrooge is the funny name Mrs. Figglehopper told us about," she said. "Devin, I think we found our main character. Come on. Let's go listen to some English accents."

We made our way through the thick fog and up to the door. It was old and wooden, with a grimy pane of glass in it. I put my hand on the knob and turned it, sounding a small door chime—*ding!*—as we entered.

Inside were two rooms. The tiny front room had a high desk in one corner. Behind the desk sat a small man in a faded coat, scribbling by candlelight in a book.

When we entered, he lifted his face in a surprised sort of way. "May I help you?"

"Hey," I said. "I'm Devin. This is Frankie. We're looking for a guy named Mr. Scrooge. Are you Mr. Scrooge or Mr. Marley?"

The man's expression turned puzzled. "Oh, I'm afraid Mr. Marley is dead."

Frankie and I looked at each other. We were thinking the same thing. Ghosts. Eeew.

"In fact Jacob Marley died seven years ago this very night," the man said. "Such a pity to die on Christmas Eve, of all days!"

"It's Christmas Eve? Already?" I asked. "Wow, zero shopping days left. The local mall must be crammed with people—"

"Devin," said Frankie, giving me a nudge.

Then I remembered. People in the books we drop into don't know anything outside their own stories. This guy had never heard of a mall. But looking at his faded clothes, I wondered if he did much shopping anyway.

The man nodded kindly. "My name is Bob Cratchit, by the way."

"So," said Frankie. "If you aren't Scrooge, then who *is*—"

"Cratchit!" a sharp voice shouted behind us. "What's going on out there!"

We whirled around and stared into the inner room.

A thin old man sat at a large black desk. His features were sharp. He had a long, pointed nose and a narrow, wiry chin. His cheeks were all shriveled up, his eyes were red, his lips were thin and blue, and his voice was sharp and grating.

When he saw us standing there, he jumped around his desk, growled like a bear, grabbed a ruler as if it were a sword, and charged at us!

"Yikes!" I cried.

"That," whispered Bob Cratchit, "is Mr. Scrooge!"

Chapter 4

"Who are you two?" Scrooge demanded.

"Frankie!" said Frankie, huddling on the floor.

"Devin!" said me, huddling right next to her, "We're here to—"

"To steal my money!" said Scrooge, his eyes blazing.

But before Scrooge could hack away at Frankie and me with that scary ruler of his, the outside door blew open and a voice called out cheerfully.

"A merry Christmas, Uncle Ebenezer! God save you!"

Scrooge screeched to a halt as a young man in a long bright coat, his face all in a glow, his cheeks all red, his eyes all sparkling, swept into the office with us.

"Merry Christmas, Uncle!" he boomed again.

Forgetting that Frankie and I were huddling on the floor, Scrooge stomped back to his desk, snarling, "Bah! Humbug!"

Scrooge's nephew laughed as he closed the door behind him. "Christmas, a humbug, Uncle? You don't mean that, I'm sure."

"I sort of think he does," I said. "He came at us with a very big ruler just now."

"I certainly do mean it!" said Scrooge, seating himself again. "Merry Christmas, bah! What reason have you to be merry? You're poor enough."

"What reason have you to be so glum?" said his nephew. "You're rich enough!"

Scrooge didn't seem to have an answer for that, so he just said, "Bah!" and followed it up with "Humbug!"

Frankie turned to me. "Well, someone's rude."

"That's enough out of you!" Scrooge growled at her.

But his nephew just laughed, helped us up, then pulled us both into Scrooge's office with him.

The old man narrowed his eyes at Frankie and me, then pursed his lips as if he'd just eaten something sour. "I've got my eye on you two, you know," he grumbled.

"It's Christmas Eve," said the nephew, pacing before Scrooge's giant desk. "Don't be angry—"

"What else can I be," replied his uncle, "when I live in such a world of nincompoops? What's Christmas, but a time for paying bills without money? A time for finding yourself a year poorer? A time for—"

"Presents!" I interrupted. "Christmas is a time for presents. And good food. And bunches of people cramming your house. And presents! And decorations and stuff all around. And did I mention presents—"

The nephew laughed suddenly, but Scrooge's eyes dwindled down to these beady black pinpoints and his fingers reached for the ruler again.

"Okay, keeping quiet now," I mumbled.

Scrooge turned to his nephew. "If I had my way, every idiot who goes about with 'Merry Christmas' on his lips should be boiled in his own pudding, and buried with a stake of holly through his heart!"

"Brutal," muttered Frankie.

"Uncle!" pleaded the nephew.

"Nephew!" returned the uncle sternly. "Keep Christmas in your own way, and let me keep it in mine!"

"Ha!" Frankie blurted out. "But you don't keep it."

Scrooge's eyes flashed. "Let me leave it alone, then!"

But his nephew wouldn't give up. "Uncle, I have always thought of Christmas as a good time, a kind, forgiving, charitable, pleasant time. It is the only time I know when people open their hearts freely to one another. It has never put a scrap of gold or silver in my pocket, but I believe that it *has* done me good, and *will* do me good, and I say, God bless it!"

In the front room, Bob Cratchit leaped immediately from his stool and began to applaud. "Hear, hear!"

Scrooge jumped up, too. But he didn't start clapping. "You!" he shouted at Cratchit. "Let me hear another sound from *you* and you'll keep Christmas by losing your job!"

Cratchit shrank back to his desk and went silent.

"Whoa, this guy just gets harsher and harsher," I said.

Frankie shivered. "No kidding. What a meanie—"

"Don't be angry, Uncle," the nephew continued. "Come and have dinner with my wife and me tomorrow. We're having a small party—"

"Never," said Scrooge, waving his nephew away as if he were a fly. "You're wasting my time. Good afternoon."

"Please come," pleaded the nephew.

"Good afternoon," said Scrooge.

"Why can't we be friends?"

"Good afternoon!" said Scrooge.

The nephew shook his head, but kept his smile.

"Well, I'll keep my holiday spirit to the last. So . . . a Merry Christmas, Uncle!"

"Good afternoon!" said Scrooge.

"And a Happy New Year!"

"Good afternoon!" shouted Scrooge.

His nephew left the room, and we followed him into Cratchit's little cell, while Scrooge slammed his office door—*blam!*

"Ah, well," said the nephew, "I came here on a mission to my Uncle Scrooge, but it seems I've failed. Still, I may wish you all a good Christmas anyway. My name is Fred, by the way."

"Thanks," said Frankie, shaking his hand and telling him our names. "Scrooge does seem like a sourpuss."

Fred nodded. "Ah, yes, but let's not lessen our own spirits this Christmas Eve." He turned to Cratchit. "How is Mrs. Cratchit and all the small, assorted Cratchits?"

"Very well, sir," said Bob.

"And the littlest boy, which one is he?"

"Tiny Tim, sir."

"Cute name," said Frankie. "So I guess he's small?"

"Quite little, our Tim is," said Cratchit.

"And how is Tim?" asked the nephew.

"We have hope he's getting better, sir," said Bob.

I didn't get what the problem was with the boy,

but I could tell just by the way that Cratchit said that, that Tim wasn't too well.

The look on Frankie's face told me she caught it, too.

I had a sudden burning desire to read ahead in the book to see if we get to meet Tim, but I didn't want to risk a story meltdown by flipping pages. Besides, my missing backpack might turn up at any second. I needed to be there when it did.

Ding! The doorbell chimed when Scrooge's nephew left, letting in the cold and, at the same time, two other men.

"Merry Christmas!" one of them piped up.

Blam! We turned around to see that Scrooge had opened his office door just to slam it again.

"Is it something I said?" asked the man.

"But all you said," said the other, "was Merry Christmas—"

Blam!

I sighed. "Yep, it was something you said!"

Chapter 5

The two men were dressed in what I guessed were nice business suits of the time, much nicer than Bob Cratchit's. They took off twin top hats and set them on his desk.

While Frankie and I secretly scanned around for traces of my backpack, Bob meekly opened the door to Scrooge's office, and the gentlemen entered.

The first one glanced at a list he was carrying. "Have I the pleasure of addressing Mr. Scrooge or Mr. Marley?"

"Jacob Marley is dead," said Scrooge, clutching his ruler again. "What do you want?"

"Yes, well, Mr. Scrooge," the second gentleman said, "at this festive time of year, a few of us are gathering some money to help the poor. Many thousands of people do not have proper food or shelter, you know."

What the man said sounded familiar. It was almost exactly what Mr. Wexler had said about the Christmas Banquet. I stopped searching for my backpack and listened at the door.

Scrooge growled. "Are there no prisons?"

The first gentleman sighed. "Oh, plenty of prisons."

"And the workhouses?" said Scrooge. "They are still open for business, I hope?"

"Yes. But I wish I could say they were not."

"Good, good!" said Scrooge. "I give money to keep the prisons and workhouses in good order. Those who have no money or a place to live must go there."

I was shocked. Not only by the things Scrooge said, but by the way he looked when he said them. He had a smile on his lips. A cold, creepy smile.

I realized then that I didn't like him much.

And he was the main character!

"Many can't go to the prisons and workhouses," said the second gentleman. "And many would rather die."

"If they would rather die," said Scrooge, "they should go ahead and do it! There are far too many people as it is. Now, gentlemen, I am busy. You know the way out!"

The two men shook their heads, picked themselves up, and left the office without another word.

"That was horrible!" said Frankie, storming into Scrooge's office. "How could you talk that way?"

"Horrible?" snapped Scrooge, that cruel smile still stuck to his lips. "On the contrary, it was excellent! I don't know who you two are, but you might learn from me how it's done!"

"How what's done?" I asked.

"How you hold on to your money!" said Scrooge. "You see, you can't *share* money. Once you give it away, you don't have it anymore. It's like . . . like . . ."

Frankie whirled around to me. "It's like cookies!"

"Yes, cookies!" said Scrooge. "Once you eat one, it's gone. Now, I suggest *you* be gone!"

Blam! He slammed the door on us again.

"Cookies?" I said. "You had to say that? So you think I'm like Scrooge?"

"You're not as grumpy," said Frankie. "Or as stingy. But it *is* Christmas. And you didn't share the cookies."

"It's the chocolate," I said. "It makes me crazy. Okay. I guess I should have shared my cookies with you, or given them to the school banquet thingy. I don't know. But until we find my backpack, none of that is going to be possible. It's not anywhere in this office. So what happens now?"

Frankie didn't have to answer. The clock did.

Dong! Dong! Dong! Dong! Dong! Dong! Dong! A deep, resounding bell rang seven times outside. If I know my math, seven chimes on a clock means seven o'clock. Somehow several hours had passed since we entered Scrooge's office. It was now the end of the long workday.

Bob Cratchit snapped down his feather pen, shut the giant book on his desk, and sprang up from his stool.

"We're closing now!" he whispered to us. "I get to go home! It's Christmas Eve!"

"Cratchit!" growled Scrooge as he snuffed the candles on his desk and came out to Bob's office. "You'll want the whole day off tomorrow, I suppose?"

"If it's convenient, sir—"

"It's not convenient!" snapped Scrooge.

Bob quaked. "Christmas comes but once a year, sir."

"A poor excuse for picking my pocket every twenty-fifth of December," said Scrooge. "Still, I suppose you must have the whole day off. But be here all the earlier the next morning."

"Oh, I shall be!"

"You had better," growled Scrooge. "Or it'll be

your last day in this office!" With that, he pulled on a coat so long and black it made him look like a bear, glared at Frankie and me, then stomped off into the street and vanished into the yellow fog.

"I can't believe it," said Frankie. "Is he the meanest guy in the universe, or just the whole world?"

"Yeah, he's one cheery guy," I added. "Oh, sorry, I mean—not!"

Bob Cratchit, however, was an actual cheery guy. In fact, he looked like he would just pop with excitement.

"Christmas Eve!" he chirped. "Oh! I can't wait!"

He tossed a thin scarf around his neck, plopped his hat on, and rushed for the door. Then he stopped.

"But, oh! Dear me! What about you two?"

I shrugged. "Hey, we're fine. We've got to go look for something anyway."

"No, no, it's cold tonight, and you two, well, I'm not sure where you live, but you're certainly not dressed for such a night as this."

"We'll be okay," said Frankie. "Really, we've got the book—"

"Here," he said. He pulled his own scarf off and wound it around Frankie's neck. Then he took an extra one off the coatrack and gave it to me.

"But, now you don't have one," said Frankie.

"Oh, but I have my family waiting for me. That will

keep me quite warm. Wait. I suddenly have a better idea. Why don't you two come home for dinner with me?"

Frankie gave me a look. A glance at the page told us the story didn't follow him. It followed Scrooge.

"Sorry, Mr. Bob," I said. "Maybe we'll hook up later."

"I do hope so! Well, until then—Merry Christmas!"

"Merry Christmas!" I said. It felt good saying it.

Bob shut up the office, then ran off down the street, sliding down the slippery walk with a bunch of boys at least twenty times before shooting off around the corner for home.

"Even if he isn't the richest guy on earth, Bob sure seems happy," said Frankie. "Lots of Christmas spirit."

"Sure, once he gets out of the office," I said. "He reminds me of me—on a Friday afternoon at bus time."

We had a chuckle over that. But even as we did, the fog and darkness got thicker, and the temperature went down even further, and we remembered what we were supposed to be doing.

Following Ebenezer Scrooge. Mr. Nice Guy. Not.

Wrapping Bob Cratchit's thin scarves around us, we passed out of the court where Scrooge and Marley's offices were, when I suddenly got a whiff of something familiar.

"Frankie, I smell cookies—"

"Chocolate cookies!" she said.

We zipped around the corner to see a row of shops, all bright on the inside, full of people, and blazing from the lamps hanging in the frosted windows.

The first was a bakery. The door opened, and a woman and her little girl left with a white bag bulging with warm baked goods and bringing the smell with them into the cold street.

I sniffed it all in, then sighed. "False alarm. Not mom's cookies. But it sure does smell good."

"Too bad we have no money," said Frankie, her face orange in the glow from the shop windows. "I am getting a bit hungry."

At that moment, a gentleman came along and flipped something shiny at us. It clanked on the street at our feet. Frankie picked it up. It was a coin.

"Hey, old-fashioned money," I said. "They think we're poor."

"Well, look at you. Ratty jeans, T-shirt, stringy hair."

I made a face. "Where I come from, it's called style."

But I knew what she meant. There we were, standing in front of food shops, hungry, shivering because we weren't dressed for the weather, and looking like we didn't belong.

"I'll keep the coin," said Frankie, popping it into her pocket. "It'll make a cool souvenir of our time in this book."

"If we ever get out of it," I said. "We already lost Scrooge. Keep the book close and let's find him."

As we made our way through the streets, we saw a group of kids whose clothes really were ragged. They had dark eyes and dirty faces, but they were singing. "God bless you, merry gentleman! May nothing you dismay!"

Then one of the singers, a boy who looked about our age, spotted a man coming up the street. Running to him, he called, "Please, sir, do you have any money to spare—"

"Bah! Humbug!" the man shouted, raising his hand.

I gasped. "It's Scrooge! We found him."

While the singers fled into the nooks and crannies of the fog, Scrooge stomped off his own way.

"Can you believe it," said Frankie, staring at Scrooge. "I think I just heard him laugh!"

"Poor kids, just trying to make a living," I said. "Frankie, I'm really worried about this Dickens guy. If he's so great, why did he make such a nasty guy the main character of a supposedly Christmas story?"

"I don't know," she said. "But I guess we better follow Scrooge anyway. He just turned a corner."

"We'll follow," I said. "But at a distance. He

might still have his attack ruler with him."

The crooked old guy made his old crooked way through the crooked streets, his head always turned down, until he came upon a gloomy dead-end alley. It was a court of what looked like office buildings towering over one small depressed-looking house.

"Pretty lonely digs," I whispered.

"I bet he likes it that way," Frankie said. "It's sad."

"And spooky," I said. "It reminds me we're in a ghost story. Just don't show me any cold white hands poking out of the fog."

There weren't any cold white hands.

But there was something else.

As Scrooge groped his way to the house, he stopped with a sudden jerk.

On the door was a large door knocker. It had a big loop of brass on the front that you bang on the door with, so that people will answer the door.

I thought it was odd that Scrooge should even have a knocker on his door. I couldn't imagine he ever got visitors. But as odd as that was, it was nothing compared to what happened next.

As Frankie and I—and Scrooge—stared at the knocker, it suddenly wasn't a knocker anymore.

It had turned into a face.

Scrooge staggered back and gasped out a name.

"Jacob Marley!"

Chapter 6

Scrooge stared at the face and said the name again.

"Jacob Marley!"

The face on the knocker—Marley's face—was old and thin and sharp, like Scrooge's, but had wire spectacles turned up on its pale forehead. The hair, what there was of it, was blown back as if by a breeze, and though the eyes were wide open, they were staring forward as if they saw nothing.

"M-M-Marley?" I whispered. "But isn't he . . . dead?"

Frankie turned to me. "If he weren't, it would be really hard to get his face into the knocker, wouldn't it?"

"You mean—"

"Ghosts," she said. "Just like the story says—"

Then even as we stared at it, the face faded into nothing, and the knocker was just a knocker again.

"Hum—humbug!" said Scrooge. Then, turning to see us again, he scowled. "Why are you two following me?"

"Um . . . we're looking for something," I said.

"You won't get my money!"

"We don't want your money," said Frankie.

"Humph!" he snorted. Then he inserted his key into the lock, pushed the door open, and stepped inside. Since the guy liked to slam doors so much, I expected him to slam this one in our faces, which would have made it tough for us to follow him through the story.

But he didn't. Maybe seeing Marley's face on the knocker had spooked him. Maybe he didn't want to be alone just then. Whatever it was, Scrooge seemed to hold the door open just long enough for us to slip inside. Then he closed the door with his usual harshness.

Boom-oom-oom! The sound resounded through the house like thunder. Every room above and every room below seemed to have a separate echo of its own.

"I don't know about anybody else, but I don't like spooky echoes," I mumbled. "Especially in the dark.

And by the way, Mr. Scrooge, you seem to have a lot of darkness around here."

"Bah!" said Scrooge. He lit a tiny candle that had been sitting on a nearby table, and headed for a wide set of stairs.

"That little candle doesn't do much," said Frankie. "What you need is some real light in this place. A couple of ceiling lamps, a string of Christmas lights, some lava lamps, maybe a tree with spotlights in the corner. Something that would brighten the house right up. I have catalogs at home that would make this place glow—"

"Humph!" snarled Scrooge, starting up the stairs. "I don't care a button for that. Darkness is cheap. I like it!"

Scrooge reached the top of the stairs and opened a door off the landing. Inside was a small, firelit sitting room. Beyond that was a bedroom, and off to the side, a room filled with logs for the fireplace.

Scrooge peered in the doorway, but didn't go in. I was sure he was remembering Marley's face again. He turned to us. "As long as you're here, go look around!"

I turned to Frankie. She nodded.

So together we searched.

"There's nothing under the table, nothing under the sofa," said Frankie.

"Nothing under the bed or in the closet, either," I said. "No backpack anywhere."

"And no ghosts!" said Scrooge. "Ha! What did I tell you? No such thing as ghosts!" He disappeared into the bedroom and returned in a long thick nightgown with a funny stocking cap dangling off his head.

"What? Are you two still here?" he said, plopping down into a chair next to the fireplace.

Both Frankie and I knew that the story followed Scrooge, and that we'd have to stay pretty close to the meanie if we were ever going to get to the end.

Frankie gulped. "Um . . . do you think . . . since you have all this room . . . and because we're kids . . . and not from around here . . . and it's cold outside . . ."

"Enough!" Scrooge snapped. "I'm not such a chatty person! Look, I get warm by the fire, then I go to sleep in my bed. I don't much care where you sleep, but I expect you gone by tomorrow morning!"

"Thank you, thank you!" I said, jumping up and down. "I'll be really quiet, and I never snore—"

"And if he does," said Frankie, "I'll poke him with a ruler. Besides, Bob Cratchit invited us to spend Christmas Day with him, anyway."

"Bob Cratchit?" Scrooge snarled. "He couldn't feed a family of mice! And Christmas? It's nothing but a—hum—hum—hum—!"

He didn't get a chance to say the rest. But even if

he had, we probably wouldn't have been able to hear him.

For at that second, though the house was empty except for us, there came a huge clanking, clanging noise from deep down below, as if somebody were dragging heavy chains around in the cellar. It thundered through the whole house.

Clank! Clong! Krreeek! Boom!

Scrooge leaped from his chair. "Ghosts!" he cried. "Ghosts! I've heard that ghosts in haunted houses are always dragging chains!"

"Ghosts!" I yelped. "Oh, no! So it's true!"

From deep down below us came a sudden, swift crashing sound, which sent Scrooge wailing, "That was the cellar door! Oh!"

But the sound didn't stop in the cellar. It was coming up the cellar stairs one by one—*boom-boom-boom*!

Then the terrible noise dragged across a lower floor. It was definitely chains and the clanking and clanging of iron boxes.

"That's really going to wreck the floors!" said Frankie.

It was getting louder and louder.

Then it came up the stairs we had just been on.

Then straight toward the sitting-room door.

"Devin!" Frankie cried out, jumping over to me.

43

"It's humbug, still!" said Scrooge defiantly. "Humbug, I say! I won't believe it!"

"You better believe it," I said. "Because, whatever it is—it's coming right here!"

The clanking, clanging noise—and the thing that was making the noise—reached the landing outside the room and, without stopping, came right on through the heavy door and passed into the room before us.

Scrooge made a sort of choking sound in his throat and spat out two words that confirmed to me that this wasn't the nice jolly snowman and sparkly presents and red-nosed reindeer kind of Christmas story.

"Marley's—ghost!" Scrooge said.

Clutching Frankie's arm, I screamed out at the top of my lungs.

"Frankie—I see dead people!"

Chapter 7

Marley's ghost.

There was no denying it. The thing had the same face as the door knocker, only it was attached to a body.

Well, a sort of body.

"Devin, he's—see-through!" Frankie hissed.

It was true. From Marley's front you could see the buttons on the back of his coat. Not only that, his hair was being blown about by that same invisible breeze that the knocker's hair did.

He wore a vest, pants, and boots. But the strangest part of his outfit, and the noisiest, was the chain.

It was thick and heavy and was locked around his

waist, and wound about behind him like a tail. Clamped to it were boxes, safes, keys, padlocks, large books, and papers and other things, all made of heavy iron.

"It's all money stuff," Frankie said, her voice quaking.

Marley's ghost dragged his heavy chain into the room with him and, though he wasn't looking at him, stopped right before Scrooge.

Scrooge himself, still glued to his chair, was shaking as bad as Frankie and me. I could hear his knees knocking and teeth chattering. "I don't believe it!" he said.

The ghost just stared ahead with death-cold eyes, his hair blown by a breeze none of us felt.

"Well!" said Scrooge finally. "W-w-what do you want with m-m-me?"

"Much!" said Marley.

The ghost barely opened his mouth, but the sound that came out was big, and echoed throughout the house as if he were yelling in a tunnel.

He stood there staring ahead while we melted into puddles on the floor. Frankie looked at me, then at Scrooge, then finally decided to speak to it.

"So, like, who—or what—*are* you?" she asked.

"Ask me who I *was*," said the ghost.

"All right, all right, who *were* you then?" Scrooge snapped.

"In life, I was your partner, Jacob Marley."

That sent a whole new round of shivers through the room. To hear him say it, meant that it really was true—he was actually the ghost of a dead guy. My ears went hot, my skin went cold. I felt sick.

The ghost just stood there.

"Can you sit down?" I asked.

"I can," said the ghost. He plopped down on the opposite side of the fireplace from Scrooge. Turning his head to look first at us, then at Scrooge, he said, "You don't believe in me."

"I don't!" said Scrooge. "You may be a bad dream, or something I ate. Ha! You could be nothing more than an undigested bit of beef! Or a crumb of cheese! Ha! You might be a fragment of an underdone potato—"

I almost laughed. "A potato ghost? So you're saying there's more *gravy* than *grave* about him!"

"Devin, don't make the dead guy mad," said Frankie.

Too late.

The spirit made a horribly loud cry, shaking its chain with such a huge noise. "Do you believe in me or not?"

"I do, I do. I must!" said Scrooge. "But why do spirits walk the earth? And why do you come to me?"

"It is required that everyone's spirit walk among

47

its fellow creatures and share its goodness with them," said the ghost. "If that spirit does not do so in life, it is condemned to do so after death!"

"But what is all that you carry around, and why do you have it?" asked Scrooge. "It can't be comfortable."

Again Marley howled and made a cry, and shook his chain and wrung his pale hands. "I wear the chain I made while I lived!" he boomed. "I made it of my own free will, and of my own free will—I wore it. Ebenezer Scrooge! Your chain was as heavy and as long as this seven Christmas Eves ago. You have worked on it since then. Oh, it is a long and terrible chain!"

We all looked around Scrooge, but saw no chain.

Then it hit me what the ghost meant. "Excuse me, Mr. Marley, are you saying that your chain is made up of all the bad things you did? And we all have chains, only we can't see them while we're alive?"

"Ah! Yes!" said Marley sadly, as if he saw Scrooge's chain growing longer by the second.

"Mark me!" said the ghost. "My time here is short. I cannot rest, I cannot stay, I cannot linger anywhere. Oh, seven long years, and yet I have such long weary journeys ahead of me!"

"You've been traveling ever since you died?" I asked.

"The whole time," said Marley. "No rest, no peace!"

"Do you travel fast?" asked Frankie.

"On the wings of the wind," replied the ghost.

"You've probably covered a lot of ground in seven years—" I said.

The ghost set up another cry and clanked its chain so loudly I thought I'd faint. But I was too scared to faint.

"At this time of the year I suffer most!" Marley went on. "Oh, why did I walk through crowds with my eyes turned down? Why did I never raise them to the star which led the Wise Men to Bethlehem?"

"You mean why didn't you ever get into the Christmas mood?" I asked. "For me, it's always my mom's special chocolate-chip cookies that jump-start the Christmas season. But now they're lost—"

"Devin?" said Frankie. "Focus. There's a story going on here, you know."

"Scrooge, hear me!" said Marley. "You still have a chance and hope of escaping my horrible fate! A chance and hope that I have arranged for you, Ebenezer!"

Scrooge perked up at that, and nearly smiled. "You were always a good friend to me, Jacob. Thank you."

"You will be haunted," said Marley, "by three spirits."

Scrooge's smile faded. "Haunted by three spirits? Oh, then, I think I'd rather not. I don't care for ghosts and goblins and such."

"Include me out, too," I said. "One ghost is plenty."

"Expect the first tomorrow, when the bell tolls one!"

"But can't we take them all at once and get it all over with?" said Frankie. "Sort of a three-for-one deal?"

The ghost's cold eyes didn't blink. "Expect the second on the next night at the same hour. The third upon the next night at the last stroke of twelve!"

When he had said this, the spirit began to walk backward away from us. What was weird was how with each step he took, the window across the room raised itself a little. By the time Marley reached it, it was wide open.

"He's going out the window," I whispered. "Ghosts really can fly. I've always wanted to fly, but not if you have to be a ghost!"

Before Marley flew out, however, he called us over with a wave of his hand. At the same time, we started to hear a bunch of strange moaning noises coming from outside. It was like a chorus of people who couldn't sing very well, but did it anyway at the top of their lungs.

Frankie clutched my arm. "I don't want to look out there. It'll be scary. I know it will be scary—"

I felt the same, but we couldn't not look.

What we saw scared us, all right.

The air outside the window was filled with phantoms, all of them rushing around, throwing their arms up, pleading and howling. Even as we watched, Marley's ghost floated out the window and joined them. Every one of them wore a chain as heavy and long as Marley's.

"I know those people!" said Scrooge, the cold night air whooshing around him. "They were all good men of business."

"I guess they went bad," I murmured.

There was one old ghost in a white vest who had a humongous safe attached to his ankle. He was crying and pleading from the air. He seemed to be trying to reach a poor woman huddled with her baby in a doorway on the street below. The snow was covering the woman, and the ghosts swarmed all around her trying to reach her, but they couldn't. And because they couldn't, they howled and screamed even louder.

"They can't do anything to help her," I said.

"It's too late for them," said Frankie, her eyes wide in fear. "Because they're all . . . dead!"

As we watched, the woman wandered off into the night, and the creatures seemed to fade into the mist and fog. Their voices faded together, and the night became as it had been when we got to Scrooge's place.

"Where did they all go?" I said.

"Never mind where they went!" snapped Scrooge with more than a touch of fear in his voice. "Gone is good enough!"

He shut the window against the cold.

"Bah—hum . . ." He couldn't get the *bug* part of his favorite saying out. He was obviously too scared.

He rushed from the sitting room to his bedroom where he leaped across the floor and into bed.

A moment later, the room filled with snores. Old Scrooge was fast asleep.

Frankie tugged the window down, then turned to me in the dark. "Devin, the author was right to call this a ghost story. We're just at the beginning and we've already seen bunches of them."

"No kidding," I said. "And I thought Christmas was a happy time. This is more like school. Marley's sending these ghosts to teach us a lesson."

"Us?" said Frankie. "You mean Scrooge? This is his story, after all."

I nodded. "Scrooge. Right. Well, should we read? And by *we* I mean *you*?"

She glanced down at the open page. "We're at the end of the chapter, but already it's getting blurry.

"So are my eyes," I said. "I wonder why."

Frankie yawned. "Maybe because we're supposed to be asleep. Because you can't wake up to a ghost if you're not asleep."

I yawned, too. "I guess."

Now, whether it was all the weirdness of ghosts, or that I had gotten less than my usual fourteen hours of sleep the night before, or the fact that I didn't know where my backpack was, or the whole Christmas Banquet problem, or the fact that I was superhungry, I don't know.

All I know is that an instant after Frankie hit the sofa, I hit the chair.

And a half-sec later, we were both fast asleep.

If Frankie was anything like me, she was having a nightmare.

Chapter 8

My nightmare was about school.

I was in the cafeteria, and Mr. Wexler was standing over me, his eyebrow wiggling with disappointment. Next to him was Mrs. Figglehopper, hands on her hips.

"Why won't you share your cookies with our Christmas Banquet?" they asked.

"They're in my backpack!" I pleaded. "I lost them!"

"That backpack must be very heavy," Mrs. Figglehopper boomed. "It's so full of things for yourself!"

Suddenly, they began to howl loudly, wailing and yelling all over the place, and throwing their arms this way and that like the spirits outside Scrooge's window. The horrible sound echoed throughout the school. The whole thing was getting very weird and crazy when the bell rang. I ran for the bus. But it wasn't the school bell.

Bong! Bong! Bong!

Suddenly, Frankie was shaking me.

"Devin, Devin, something's happening. Wake up!"

I yanked myself out of my nightmare, and there I was in Scrooge's room again, listening to the chimes of a nearby church ringing the hour.

The room was so dark you could barely tell the grimy window from the grimy wall. Scrooge was there, of course, sitting up in bed, rubbing his beady eyes.

Bong! Bong! Bong! The heavy-sounding bell went on from six to seven, from seven to eight, and all the way to twelve, then stopped.

"This is nonsense," said Scrooge, wiggling his pinkies in his ears. "It was at least two o'clock in the morning whcn we fell asleep."

"Hey, it's 1843," I said. "I bet you guys don't even have digital yet. Maybe an icicle got stuck in the clock."

Scrooge lit a candle by his bed. "And maybe we dreamed the whole thing. Maybe ghosts don't exist!" He scrambled to the window and rubbed the frost off with the sleeve of his robe. "I see no ghosts out there."

"Marley said we would be visited by the first

spirit at one in the morning," said Frankie, tapping the page where it said that. "That's an hour from now. It's weird having an appointment with a ghost, but we may as well stay up. I'll read for a bit."

While Frankie read, I tried to get the fire going in the fireplace, but it was hopeless. "Man, if you're so rich, and your rooms are so cold, how do other people live?"

"It's not my business," said Scrooge.

"Nice Christmas spirit," Frankie mumbled, looking up from the book.

I thought again of that poor lady with the baby who the ghosts wanted to help. She shouldn't be outside on a night like this. If the ghosts couldn't help her, somebody should. Scrooge sure wouldn't. Then who?

Ding-dong! went the church's quarter-hour bell.

"A quarter past the hour," said Scrooge.

Ding-dong!

"Half past!"

Ding-dong!

"A quarter to the hour," said Scrooge.

Ding-dong!

"The hour itself," said Scrooge. "And nothing else! You see, ha, ha! There are no such things as ghosts! It was all our silly imaginations, running away with us. Why, ghosts are nothing but a hum—"

Even before he finished his favorite expression, the hour bell sounded a deep, dull, booming *ONE*.

And even before it finished sounding, light flashed up in the room, and suddenly we were not alone.

Frankie and I gasped at the same time. "Oh!"

Scrooge looked as if he were going to swallow his whole head in fear. "Oh, dear me!"

A strange figure stood before us.

It was like a small child, sort of, and sort of like an old man. Its hair was long and white, but the face was smooth and not at all wrinkly. The arms were long and muscle-y and so were the legs. It wore some kind of old-style tunic, all white, and a belt that was lit up with twinkly clear lights.

In its hand was a branch of green holly like you see at Christmastime, but the tunic was decorated with the kind of summer flowers my mom grows in her garden.

But the weirdest part of all was that from the top of the creature's head there shone a steady stream of light, as if it had a spotlight up there. This is what was lighting up the room. Under its arm was a big metal cone, like a candle snuffer, just about the right size to go over its head.

All in all, it didn't look like an attack ghost, but I still wasn't going to run over and give it a hug.

Scrooge was the first to speak. "Are you the spirit whose coming was foretold to me?"

"I am," said the spirit. Its voice was soft, but sounded as if it came into the room from a long distance.

"Who—and what—are you?" asked Frankie.

"I am the Ghost of Christmas Past."

"Long past?" asked Scrooge.

"No. Your past." The spirit nodded its head at Scrooge as it said the last two words.

I pointed to the metal cone under the ghost's arm. "What's that?"

"My cap," said the spirit. "But we have miles to go before my light is put out. Scrooge, take heed, rise, and walk with me!" It put out its strong hand and clasped Scrooge by the arm.

"Is it all right if we tag along?" I asked. "We sort of have to. There's this whole thing about being in a book and us trying to find a backpack and stuff, which you probably won't understand—"

The spirit turned to me with a smile that seemed to say it *did* understand, and that it was okay for us to go with them. But when it stepped toward that window again, the one Marley had floated out of, Frankie and I screeched to a stop.

"What is it?" asked the spirit.

"Well, it's sort of a problem we have with heights,"

I said. "We fall down from them. I mean, guys like you and Marley can float out of all the windows you want, but Frankie and I are just regular folks. We go *splat*—"

"Right," said Frankie. "So if you can just wait a sec we'll meet you downstairs. . . ."

Without losing its smile, the spirit said, "Touch my hand, and you shall be upheld with me!"

Scrooge's look said that even though he was Mr. Cranky, he wanted us to go with him. So I said, "Okay."

As soon as we touched the spirit's sleeve, all four of us passed right through the wall—or maybe the wall dissolved—whatever it was, we were suddenly standing on an old country road somewhere.

"London's gone," said Frankie. "It just vanished."

The darkness and mist had vanished, too, and it was a clear, cold, winter day in the country. There were fields on either side of the road, all dusted with snow.

"So where are we?" I asked.

Scrooge jumped. "Why—I—I was a boy here!"

Chapter 9

"Oh, dear! Oh, my! It was so long ago!" Scrooge said, fairly hopping up and down on the old road.

"Do you remember the way?" the spirit asked softly.

"Remember it?" cried Scrooge. "I could walk it blindfolded! Let's go. Come along, everyone. Follow me!"

Still in his robe and nightcap and slippers, Scrooge bolted off, skipping and prancing over the rough road.

"He moves pretty quick for an old guy," I said.

"So I guess we'd better follow him," said Frankie.

As he bopped along, Scrooge pointed out every stone, every tree, every gate and fence he remembered. When some boys appeared, riding shaggy ponies and calling to one another as they rode away from a small village, Scrooge nearly burst with delight.

"Ho, there!" he yelled out. "Boys! Stop! Ho, boys!"

The Spirit of Christmas Past touched Scrooge lightly on the arm. "These are shadows of the past, shades of things that once were. Those boys do not know we are here."

Even so, Scrooge called out the boys' names one by one. "Why, there's David Fieldercop! And Nicholas Bickleny! Oh, and my dear friend, Martin Wizzlechut!"

I laughed. "Hey, Frankie. Remember Mrs. Figglehopper told us how the author likes to give his characters funny names—"

The spirit smiled. "Mrs. Figglehopper? Ah, now, that's a funny name."

Scrooge's eyes glistened to see his old friends as they wished one another a Merry Christmas, then parted at the crossroads and trotted off to their homes. But his smiles faded as he spotted a dark snow-dusted mansion in the distance. "My old school," he muttered.

"The school is not quite deserted," said the ghost. "A single boy remains there, forgotten by his friends."

"I know it," said Scrooge.

We touched the spirit's sleeve again, and we were inside the school.

The rooms were huge and cold, with broken desks in the classrooms and dark, stained walls.

Dust covered the floors, and there was a funny smell, too, which reminded me a little too much of a zoo and not enough like a school.

"Makes you appreciate Palmdale a bit more," I said.

"A whole lot more," Frankie agreed.

The ghost led us to a door at the back. It opened onto a long, bare room of empty desks. In the shadows a small boy was sitting, a book spread out before him.

"Hi," I said. The boy didn't look up.

"Devin, he can't hear you or see you," said Frankie.

Which was too bad, because the kid, who seemed around ten years old, definitely looked as if he could use some company.

"Books were my only friends," said Scrooge, his eyelids flicking away what I'm pretty sure were tears. "Books were my only companions during the Christmases I spent here alone."

"This is brutal," said Frankie. "You had to spend Christmas all alone? At school?"

"You must have been really bad," I said.

He turned to us. "Bad? No. My father didn't like me, that's all . . . oh! Poor Ebenezer! Poor boy!"

I glanced at Frankie. "Ouch . . ."

She shook her head sadly.

Scrooge sat down next to his small self and looked at him closely. "I wish, I wish, but, no, it's too late now."

"What is the matter?" asked the spirit.

"Nothing," said Scrooge. "Nothing. There was a boy singing a Christmas song on the street last night. I wish I had given him something, that's all."

Frankie pulled from her pocket the coin we had gotten from the man in the street. "It's called charity."

The ghost smiled thoughtfully, then waved its hand. "Let us see another Christmas, Ebenezer Scrooge!"

It happened in an instant.

Scrooge's former self suddenly grew larger, and the room around us became even darker and more dirty. The windows cracked, bits and chunks of plaster fell from the ceiling, the floor became more stained and dull, and the dust mounted up like mini–snow drifts.

It must have been three or four Christmases later, and kid Scrooge was still there. But he wasn't reading. He was pacing up and down the classroom.

"He's waiting for someone," said Frankie.

And someone did come.

The door behind us opened, and a little girl, much younger than the boy, came darting in.

"Dear brother!" she exclaimed. "I have come to bring you home, dear brother! To bring you home! Home!"

The girl put her arms around young Scrooge and hugged him and gave him a kiss.

Young Scrooge's eyes welled with tears. "Home, little Fan? No, it can't be—"

"But it is!" she said. "Yes! Home, once and for all. Home, for ever and ever. Father is so much kinder than he used to be, and he spoke so gently to me one night that I wasn't afraid to ask once more if you might come home. And he said yes, you *should* come home—right away. And he sent me in a coach to bring you!"

"But, Fan . . . I can't believe it!" young Scrooge said.

"You are never to come back here, Ebenezer. Ever, as long as you live. And we'll be together all Christmas long, and have the merriest time in all the world!"

Tears now streamed down young Scrooge's face. Down mine, too, and Frankie's, and even old Scrooge's.

"It's true," said Scrooge. "She did come one year,

my little Fan. And I never did come back here—"

The sound of clopping hooves from outside told us that a carriage had arrived. Fan clapped her hands and laughed as she and her brother rushed out the door together.

"She was always a delicate creature," the ghost said. "But she had a good heart."

"The very best heart in the world," said Scrooge, watching his young self step into the carriage. "The best in the whole world!"

"And when she died," said the ghost, "she had, I think, children."

"One child," said Scrooge.

"True," said the ghost. "Your nephew!"

Scrooge frowned at the floor. "My nephew."

At that moment, someone called out, "Bring down Master Scrooge's things!"

A small box was tossed down from an upper floor to the carriage driver outside. Following it came a large sack, then something purple with straps and zippers.

I nearly jumped out of my skin. "Oh, my gosh! Frankie! My backpack! It's here!"

I flew past the ghost and jumped out the door to grab my pack from the pile of stuff on the carriage.

But even as I did—and even as I smelled the

wonderful chocolaty smell of my mother's cookies—the ghost said, "Now look upon yet another Christmas, Ebenezer Scrooge!"

"Not yet!" I shouted. "My backpaaaaack—"

But the spirit wouldn't wait. With a wave of its hand, the school was gone, and the countryside began to fade.

"Wait!" I yelled.

I actually felt the strap in my hand when all of a sudden an old-fashioned buckled shoe came out of nowhere and kicked the pack out of my fingers.

It didn't skitter across the snowy ground but across a wooden floor and into the shadows of a large room.

"Hey!" I yelled. "Who's kicking?!"

Scrooge laughed suddenly. "Why, it's Mr. Fezziwig!"

Chapter 10

The strange buckled shoe, and another one just like it, clacked across the wooden floor, kicking my backpack with each swinging foot. *Whack! Whump!*

"Don't do that!" I said. "I got cookies in there!"

"Why, it's old Fezziwig!" said Scrooge, clapping his hands in delight as a plump old man made his way to a high desk at the end of the room, seeming not to know he was kicking a purple backpack with every step.

"Frankie, Devin, look! It's old Fezziwig, alive again!"

"Alive and kicking my cookies to smithereens!" I yelled. "Frankie, help me—"

But even as we charged across the floor toward

the pack, a strange, skinny hand thrust itself out of the shadows—a pale, white, ghostly hand, just like the one before!—and snatched the bag away. It vanished into nothing.

Frankie slid to a stop. "Oh, my gosh! That was so weird."

"Told you!" I cried. "This book is jammed with ghosts and some of them like to steal stuff. Cookie thieves—"

"Ha, ha!" Scrooge laughed again. "Frankie, Devin, look. I worked here as a young man. Come quickly!"

"The backpack will turn up later," said Frankie, tapping the book. "Then we'll be ready for it. In the meantime, let's stick with the story."

Grumbling, I turned around to see that we were in what looked like a warehouse, piled high with boxes of all sizes. Yet, it was obviously Christmastime again. Frost covered the windows, and you could hear the cold wind howling outside. But inside, evergreen garlands hung from the walls, and candles blazed cheerily in every corner.

"This is actually pretty cozy," Frankie said.

"It's wonderful!" said Scrooge. "And now—"

Da-dong! The clock on the wall chimed the hour.

Mr. Fezziwig, who was seated atop his high desk, glanced at the clock, grinned, then laid down his pen.

"Yo-ho there, Ebenezer! Hilli-ho, Dick! Come!"

Clambering in from the back came Scrooge's former self, older and taller than before, looking to be about high-school age. With him was another boy.

"Yo-ho, my boys!" said Fezziwig, chortling as he climbed down from his desk to join the boys. "No more work tonight. Christmas Eve, Dick. Christmas, Ebenezer!"

"Shall we close the shutters, sir?" asked young Scrooge politely.

"Close the shutters!" said Fezziwig. "Then shove the desks and tables over to the side. Throw more logs on the fire. And bring in the food! It's Christmas!"

Scrooge and Dick were a blur of laughing activity. They dashed into the street and closed the shutters. The tables and desks were whisked away in a flash. And platters and bowls and pots and pans heaped with steaming food were brought in with help from the even more plump Mrs. Fezziwig.

"Here comes the DJ," Frankie said with a chuckle, when a guy as thin as the violin under his arm came in.

The instant he started sawing at the thing, Mrs. Fezziwig's toes started tapping. She called in three girls as round as their mother and, stumbling after them, six young men arguing over who would get the first dance.

Soon, bunches of people flooded out of the back

rooms and before you knew it, it was a blazing party.

"This guy Fezziwig sure knows how to throw a bash," said Frankie.

"Indeed he does," said Scrooge, clapping his hands.

In the blazing light, Frankie read, and I laughed. Then she laughed, and I read. My backpack didn't turn up in Fezziwig's warehouse, but it was one awesome party.

Even though the bash went on for four hours, it zipped by in the book. Four hours of thirty people hopping and spinning and rushing around doing old-time dances. Four hours in six pages, then it was over!

Da-dong! The clock struck eleven, and the music stopped, and Mr. and Mrs. Fezziwig laughed their way to the door, taking up positions on either side of it. They shook hands with everyone, wished everyone a merry Christmas, and sent them cheerily on their way.

During the whole thing, old Scrooge acted like a kid in a toy store. He pointed everywhere, remembering this person, that song, his eyes glistening nearly as much as his young self's.

After the last person left, the spirit turned to him, the light on its head burning more bright and clear than ever. "Why do you take such delight from the scene? It cost Fezziwig nearly nothing."

"Pah! It isn't that!" snapped Scrooge. "It isn't the money. Fezziwig had the power to make us happy, and he did. That joy was as great as if it had cost a fortune. . . ."

He stopped.

"What is the matter?" asked the ghost.

"Nothing," said Scrooge, frowning. "Except that I should like to be able to say a word to my own clerk, Bob Cratchit, just now. That's all. Just a word."

"Not a nasty word, like you were telling him before?" I said. "Because you were sort of harsh, you know."

"No, no, " said Scrooge. "A kind word, if he would listen."

"Come," said the ghost. "My time grows short!"

An instant later, we were huddled in the corner of a small room in a house somewhere.

Before us sat a young woman. In her eyes, which sparkled in the light shining from the Ghost of Christmas Past, there were tears.

Young Scrooge was there, but older now, and nearly grown up. He was pacing across the room in front of the woman, snorting to himself.

"I don't understand," he was saying, "I don't—"

"Ebenezer," said the woman softly. "You do not

love me anymore. Another idol has taken my place in your heart. A golden one. You love money more than you love me."

"Uh-oh," I whispered. "Love troubles. This isn't my thing. I'm gonna scout around for you-know-what—"

"Stay and listen!" hissed Frankie. "This is important."

Young Scrooge grunted under his breath. "I merely want to be rich so that the world will not drag me down. I refuse to be poor! The world is cruel to the poor!"

"Ebenezer, you fear the world too much," said the woman, more tears flooding her eyes. "When you said you loved me, you were another man—"

"Bah! I was a boy," he said impatiently.

"Your own words tell me you were not what you are now," she said. "Therefore . . . I release you."

She pulled a small ring off her finger.

"Oh, this is cruel!" young Scrooge protested, snatching the ring and stomping across the room, standing suddenly side by side with his older self.

"Look at him," Frankie whispered. "He's so different now from when he was with his sister, or at Fezziwig's."

Seeing them there together, one in the past, one in the present, it was clear that Frankie had hit on something. The younger Scrooge no longer smiled as he had at Fezziwig's party. There was an icy glint in his eyes that scared me. He was so much more like the Scrooge who was mean to his nephew. The one who forced the charity guys to go away. The old grouch who yelled at the poor boy singing in the street.

Already, he loved money more than anything else.

"So, you release me?" young Scrooge asked sharply. "Even though I shall soon have great wealth?"

"Wealth is not love," said the woman. "Go. I hope you will be happy in the life you have chosen—"

"Thank you! I shall be!" snapped Scrooge.

"And a merry Christmas to you, Ebenezer—"

"Humbug!" he said, then stormed out of the room, slamming the door behind him.

"So," I said to old Scrooge, "is this where you learned to slam doors?"

"Spirit, take me from this place!" Scrooge demanded.

"I have told you, these are shadows of the things that have been," said the spirit softly. "Do not blame me if they are unpleasant to you. We shall see more!"

"No!" said Scrooge. Then his eyes flashed as he saw that the spirit's light was burning high and bright. "So, your brightness means you have power over me? Then I will put that light out! And you will haunt me no more!"

"No!" said Frankie. "Don't mess with ghosts!"

But Scrooge seized the big cone-shaped extinguisher hat that the spirit carried with him, and pressed it down suddenly upon the ghost's head. "There!"

The ghost dropped beneath it, so that the cone covered his head. But even Scrooge couldn't hide the spirit's light. It shone all over the ground under the cap.

"Frankie, let's help the ghost!" I said.

Together we seized the cone and tried to pull it back off the nice spirit's head, but Scrooge was too strong for even the three of us. Soon the struggle was over.

The spirit's light went out.

Things went misty and dark for an instant, then we were in Scrooge's room again.

"That was not good," I said. "Not good at all."

"Humbug!" shouted Scrooge. Then, exhausted from his struggle, he breathed heavily and fell onto his bed.

In a moment, he was deep asleep.

It being too dark to read, and too cold to stay awake, and seeing that not much would happen until Scrooge woke up, Frankie curled up in the chair and I tumbled onto the sofa. Like Scrooge, I was fast asleep before my head hit the cushions.

Chapter 11

"Grrrr-sss! Grrrr-sss!" Someone was snoring big time.

"Grrrr-sss! Grrrr-sss!" It was really annoying.

"Devin—wake up!"

"Grrrr-snf-snk—what?" I woke up just in time to hear the church bell chime a deep single *BONG*!

Scrooge bolted up out of bed. "Was that all a dream, or did it actually happen? Did we really travel in the past with a spirit?"

"I'm pretty sure we did," said Frankie. "And I'm not sure you should have treated the ghost like that."

"Right," I added. "There are probably rules for dealing with ghosts with lights on their heads, and I'm sure snuffing out the light is not at the top of the list."

Scrooge frowned. "Perhaps, but now it's time for our second messenger. And let me say, nothing between a baby and a rhinoceros would surprise me very much—oh, dear, look at that!"

It was then that we noticed a powerful red light streaming under the door to Scrooge's sitting room.

Even as we noticed the light, a deep and echoey voice boomed, "Come in! Come in!"

We all stared at one another, but for some reason, we all did what the huge voice said. I think we were too scared not to.

Scrooge slid from bed, wrapped his robe tight around him, put on his slippers, and went to the door. Frankie was second. I was last.

We opened the door to an astounding sight.

Frankie gasped. "Someone remodeled last night!"

It was true. Scrooge's dingy little sitting room was completely changed. The walls and ceiling were hung so thickly with evergreen garlands that it looked like a forest in there. Bright, gleaming holly trees filled the corners of the room, and their red berries flashed and twinkled in the light of a roaring blaze in the fireplace.

Heaped up on the floor to make a weird kind of throne were plump turkeys, geese, chunks of beef, strings of sausages, dozens of pies and puddings, mounds of hot chestnuts, bright pyramids of oranges, pears, and apples, stacks and stacks of giant cakes, and enormous steaming bowls of hot punch.

And sitting on this crazy throne was a jolly giant.

"Come in!" he boomed. "Come in, and know me better! Come in! Come in!"

The creature was seven or eight feet tall and dressed in a long robe of deep green trimmed with white fur.

In his hand he held a great horn with a fire blazing in it, and on his head was a thick wreath of holly from which gleaming icicles hung. His hair was long and brown and curly, and so was his enormous beard.

We shook and trembled all over the place, but that only seemed to make him laugh more.

"Come in, Scrooge! Come in, Frankie and Devin!" boomed the giant. "I am the Ghost of Christmas Present! Look upon me and wonder!"

I nudged Frankie. "I wonder, all right. I wonder how a giant could fit in this tiny room. Not a bad trick for a ghost. And a not too spooky ghost, either."

The giant's laugh echoed around the room as if we were all in some kind of cave. "You have never seen anything like me before!" he boomed.

"I'm pretty sure we would have remembered," said Frankie. "You're . . . pretty memorable!"

Scrooge bowed before the ghost. "Spirit, take us

where you will. I learned a lesson last night. Let me learn more."

"Then touch my robe!" said the ghost.

We did, and instantly the room vanished. *Poof!* The room, and all that awesome food, gone in a flash.

We stood in the street, and with just a single glance I could tell that it was Christmas morning.

Snow lay fresh on all the rooftops, and people were everywhere, shoveling their walks clear.

The grocery shop at the corner was jammed with customers. They tumbled against one another at the door, clashing their wicker baskets wildly, some calling to others, some wishing each other a merry Christmas, everything smelling so good.

"I love this!" said Frankie, breathing it all in. "The snow and the cold, the food smells, the people. This is like Christmas really should be!"

Suddenly, a snowball whizzed past my ear.

Without thinking, I packed my own and shot it right back. But to my amazement, it hit a small boy.

"Hey!" he yelled.

"Sorry!" I said. "I thought you were a shadow—"

"A shadow, eh? I'll get you back!" he said in a miniature English accent. And he did, sending a good fastball that plastered me. I lobbed another couple back, and so did he, laughing louder with each one.

Frankie turned to the ghost. "I thought the people here were shadows."

"Scrooge and I are the shadows," said the ghost. "You can be seen, we cannot."

"It probably has something to do with being in the present," said Frankie.

I grinned. "Which means I might actually be able to get my hands on my pack—if we find it."

"Come," said the ghost. "We move on. Quickly!"

He turned the corner and entered a side lane, where a bakery was nearly bursting with people trying to get in and out.

As customers left the shop, the spirit lifted the covers off their dinners, and sprinkled something from his torch over the food. He also sprinkled it over a couple of women who were arguing about their place in line. At once, the women stopped arguing, hugged, and wished each other a merry Christmas.

"Wow," said Frankie. "Useful stuff you have in that torch. I guess you'd call it Christmas spirit . . . Spirit?"

The jolly giant just waved us on, chuckling to himself.

Frankie and I lobbed one more round of snowballs at the kid, got fully pelted in return, then slid down the street after Scrooge and the ghost.

We zigzagged our way into some snowy alleys and

stopped before the smallest, poorest house on the block.

"Spirit," said Scrooge, a tinge of fear in his voice, "why do you bring me here? I do not know this place."

"Of course, you don't," said the spirit. "Yet, it is the home of someone very close to you."

"Close to me?" said Scrooge, completely clueless. "But I don't know anyone—"

The spirit sighed. "Do you know Bob Cratchit? He lives here!"

Scrooge looked over the house, astonished that anyone could live in such a tiny place. But he was even more surprised when the spirit tossed a twinkling, glittering handful of incense on the Cratchit house.

It suddenly smelled like every good food I'd ever had. I breathed it all up. It smelled so Christmas-y.

"Is there a particular flavor in what you sprinkle from your torch?" asked Scrooge.

"There is. Something of my own."

"Too bad you can't bottle it," said Frankie.

"Would it work for any dinner?" Scrooge asked.

"To any dinner that is given in kindness," the spirit replied. "But to a poor one most."

"Why to a poor one most?" I asked.

"Because a poor one needs it most. Let us enter."

Chapter 12

The ghost went in first, leading with his magical torch. It was really cramped in the Cratchit house, and the ceilings were very low. But, amazingly, the Ghost seemed to stuff himself in there without busting a hole through the roof.

"He's pretty good at that," I whispered to Frankie.

"Christmas spirit fits in any kind of room," she said.

I looked at her. "Very deep, Frankie. And smart, too."

She grinned and handed the book to me. "It's all in here. Try reading some."

As I scanned the page we were on, Scrooge slid in next to the ghost and gazed around, shocked at the smallness of the rooms inside. "Cratchit lives *here*?"

"And his large family, too," said the ghost.

Finally, Frankie and I stepped in, and a woman about as old as my mom hustled to greet us. From her description in the book, I knew right away it was Mrs. Cratchit. Her dress was worn and tattered, but she smiled just like Bob.

"Merry Christmas, my dears! Can I help you?"

Frankie and I looked for the spirit, but he had already pulled Scrooge off to explore the house.

I turned back to Mrs. Cratchit. "Um, we thought we'd stop by to, um, that is, what I mean to say is . . ."

"We came to drop off Mr. Cratchit's scarves!" said Frankie, unwinding the scarf from her neck and handing it to the lady.

"Oh, you know my Bob!" said Mrs. Cratchit.

"We met him at the office," I said.

At this time, a stampede of smaller assorted Cratchits burst into the room from a closet in the back that was probably their room. They blasted right through old Scrooge on their way to their mother.

I recognized the kids right off from the way Dickens described them in the book. There was Peter, the oldest, Belinda in the middle, and two little Cratchit twins, a boy and a girl.

They were all talking pretty excitedly about the

big Christmas dinner that they couldn't wait to start eating.

"If you are friends of my Bob," said Mrs. Cratchit, "then you must stay for Christmas dinner! You must!"

"Please stay for dinner!" all the children chimed in.

Frankie took a deep breath. "I am getting hungry. . . ."

"Time out," I said. I pulled her aside. "The book doesn't say we stay for supper. What should we do?"

At this moment, the ghost and Scrooge came back into the room. Scrooge still had a shocked look on his face.

"Spirit," I whispered, "Is it okay if we hang here for a while? Mrs. Cratchit wants us to stay for supper."

The spirit beamed. "So, even though their dinner is small, they wish to share it? Scrooge take note!"

"Can we please stay for supper?" Frankie asked. "I mean, you and Scroogey can be shadows and all that, plus Scrooge is so thin he probably doesn't eat much, but Dev and I need to chow."

A fresh whiff of Christmas dinner suddenly entered our nostrils and even the ghost breathed it in.

"Besides," I added, "my backpack is lost somewhere in this story, maybe in this house, so we should stay and try to find it, don't you think?"

The ghost chuckled. "All right, all right, let us stay

and see their feast. Scrooge, behold. Even a poor dinner can be a happy one!"

I turned to Mrs. Cratchit and said, "Yes! We'd love to have dinner with you and the assorted Cratchiteers!"

The children cheered, "Hooray!"

"How can we help?" asked Frankie.

Mrs. Cratchit put us to work right away. In the kitchen we helped Peter blow on the small fire to keep the potatoes boiling. Soon the water got all bubbly and we heard the potatoes knocking at the saucepan lid.

Then we helped Belinda and the Cratchit twins set the table. Even though there were so many of us crowded into the small dining room, it was actually kind of fun that way. The Cratchits made us feel right at home.

Just as everything was ready, the front door was flung open. All the kids gave a cheer as Bob Cratchit rushed in.

We ran over too, then stopped.

On Bob's shoulder was a thin little boy with iron braces on his legs. In his hands he carried a little crutch.

I could feel Frankie go stiff. "We were right," she whispered. "There is something wrong with the littlest Crachit."

It was something serious, too. The boy was so frail he needed the crutch to walk. But he giggled when he hopped from his father's shoulder and was carried off by his brothers and sisters to sit by the blazing fire.

"Devin! Frankie!" said Bob, turning to us, his face all red from running. "I'd like you to meet my son—"

I suddenly remembered the conversation between Bob Cratchit and Scrooge's nephew. I jumped. "Oooh! Oooh! Wait, don't tell us! I know this from before! His name has something to do with being sort of small, right?"

Bob chuckled merrily. "It's—"

"No, no," said Frankie. "Don't tell me. I know—your name is . . . Small Sam!"

The boy giggled and shook his head. "No, it's—"

"Wait, wait!" said Frankie. "Is it . . . Puny Pete?"

"I should hope not."

"Little Larry?" I said.

"Nooooo!"

Through all these, the boy laughed and shook his head. All the other Cratchits did, too.

Frankie sighed. "I'm out. Unless it's Nutshell Nick?"

"I was going to say that!" I said.

Still laughing, the boy said, "My name is Tiny Tim!"

"I was going to say that next!" I said.

Everyone laughed again, then the older kids carried Tim into the kitchen to listen to the pudding bubbling.

When the room was quiet, Mrs. Cratchit turned to Bob by the fire. "And how did Tim behave?"

"As good as gold, and better," said Bob. "Sometimes he gets thoughtful sitting by himself so much. He told me, coming home from church, that he hoped the people saw him because he was a cripple. He said it might be pleasant to them to remember upon Christmas Day who made lame beggars walk and blind men see."

Bob's voice shook when he told Mrs. Cratchit, "I think Tim is getting better, my dear. Yes, he's getting better."

Mrs. Cratchit's silence said something else.

I glanced up at the ghost. He was looking at Scrooge.

About a minute of uncomfortable quiet was broken finally by the tapping little crutch of Tim himself, on the floor. "It's time!" he cried. "Time for supper!"

In a flash, we were packed around the table tighter than sardines. There was a little bit of everything to go around: goose, potatoes, beans, stuffing, gravy, apple sauce, and finally the famous Cratchit plum pudding.

Frankie and I stuffed ourselves so much, we had to get up and walk between courses. While we did, we poked around for my backpack, but it wasn't there.

Finally Bob raised his glass and said, "A merry Christmas to us all, including our guests! God bless us!"

The whole family echoed the toast.

"God bless us every one!" said Tiny Tim, last of all.

When he said it, Bob held Tim's small hand tightly, as if he feared it would be taken from him.

Scrooge, who had been hovering over the table, finally spoke. "Spirit, tell me about Tiny Tim."

The ghost turned. "I see an empty seat by the fireplace. And a crutch without an owner, carefully preserved. If what we see now goes unchanged by the future, the child will die."

I felt as if I'd been punched in the stomach.

"Ghost, tell us Tim will not die," said Scrooge.

"If these shadows remain unchanged, he shall!"

"But Spirit, no, please tell me—"

"We move on!" said the ghost sharply.

Frankie and I barely said our good-byes to the Cratchits, when we were suddenly far outside the city in a dark, lonely valley sunk between high jagged hills.

"Where are we now?" I asked.

"This is a place where miners live," said the spirit. "They work in the dark and dangerous depths of the earth. But they know me here. Listen!"

There was a faint sound of someone singing.

"They sing carols to me!" said the spirit. Touching his cloak, we flew across the valley and through the walls of a small hut, where a cheerful bunch of folks were huddled around a glowing fire.

We clung to the shadows in the corner, which was okay, because there wasn't really room for anyone else around the fire, and Frankie and I didn't know all the words to the songs they were singing.

They finished one old carol, laughed, wished Merry Christmases all around, then sang another.

It was nice, but before long—*whoosh!*—we were on our way again. This time, the ghost flew us straight out over the water, far away to a sailing ship that crashed and dipped on the waves.

"Even far out here, they know me," said the spirit.

There were a few men on deck, and every one of them hummed a Christmas tune or told a Christmas story.

"The Christmas spirit is everywhere," said Frankie. "This is so cool."

Actually, not so cool.

The ship rocked suddenly, and the awesome

Cratchit dinner jiggled in my stomach. I groaned. "Big meal—lots of stuffing—about to be unstuffed—Spirit, I don't do ships—or sea stuff—can we leave—"

"Very well," he said. "But it means we fly again."

"Anything but ships!" I said, as the ship rocked again. And away we flew, away through the dark and cold of the night, soaring over the ocean and back over land.

"We should be able to get our pilots' licenses after all this flying!" said Frankie, stretching her arms wide and enjoying herself.

Finally, descending into the thick darkness and biting cold and yellow fog of London once again, we heard the most sudden and unexpected thing.

Someone, very near us in the darkness, gave out a big, hearty, booming, echoing laugh—"Ha, ha! Ha, ha, *ha!*"

Chapter 13

"Ha, ha!" came the bright laugh again.

"Hey, I'm pretty sure we've heard that laugh before," said Frankie. "Who is it?"

The ghost waved his torch over us, and with a breeze that smelled like roasted turkey, the black air evaporated, and we found ourselves in a bright, gleaming room.

"Isn't this better than some smelly old boat?" I said.

All the walls and halls around us were decked with holly, every candle in the place was lit and blazing, and right there in the middle of everything was Scrooge's nephew Fred, bent over, laughing his head off.

And so was the pretty woman next to him.

"Ha-ha-ha! Ha-*ha*!"

"Scrooge, behold your nephew and his wife," said the spirit, "your niece by marriage, whom you've never met! They have no great wealth, but they know how to celebrate Christmas!"

They sure did! In that dazzling room were a dozen other jolly, fresh-faced people, and all of them had plates or glasses, and all of them were laughing, too.

The nephew turned and spotted Frankie and me by the door. "Dear, dear!" he said. "The two children from Scrooge's office! Well, come in, you two! Come in!"

Frankie grinned, then whispered to me, "Isn't it strange how so many people around Scrooge know how to have a good time, but he doesn't?"

"Good one," I agreed. "Let's hope Scrooge puts that on his list of things to fix. But in the meantime— let's party!"

The nephew introduced us all around. "As these two can tell you, Uncle Scrooge said that Christmas was a humbug. And he believed it, too!"

"Shame on him, Fred!" said Scrooge's niece. She had curly hair, bright eyes, and was really kind of cute.

"He's a comical old fellow," said Fred.

"He's very rich, for sure," I said.

"What of that?" said Fred. "He may have a million pounds, but he doesn't do anything good with it."

"He hates to give any away," said Frankie. "I bet he never gave any to you, for instance."

"Ha!" Fred exploded. "Quite right about that!"

"I have no patience with him," said Scrooge's niece.

"Oh, I have," said Fred. "I feel sorry for him. I couldn't be mad at him if I tried. He really only hurts himself. And misses out on a truly delectable Christmas dinner."

"The more for us!" yelled someone in the back.

At that, Scrooge's niece began to play on a harp, and sang a nice old-fashioned song in a pretty decent voice.

"Ah!" said Scrooge, tucking himself behind the spirit. "I remember that tune. My sister, Fan, knew that song. I heard her sing it often when I was young. . . ."

He paused, then began to cry. "Oh, dear, dear, Fan!"

The ghost looked closely at Scrooge. "The memories of a sister . . . yes, yes, she was a tender soul."

Frankie let out a deep sigh. "You know, Devin, Scrooge was mean, really mean to his nephew, but I sort of feel sorry for him now. I mean, he really did love his sister a lot."

I nodded. "Yeah. It makes you wonder if he had been with her more, and had heard her sing more often, maybe he wouldn't have grown up so mean, you know?"

I suddenly wondered, What if things were different, and there were no Frankie to have fun with? How would I be? No Frankie? Now that's a scary thought!

"Come, there is more yet to see," said the ghost.

"Not yet, spirit, please." Scrooge wiped his eyes, and began tapping his feet. "I want to stay just a little longer. Look, they are playing games!"

The first was called Yes and No. Fred started by thinking of something, and the rest of us had to guess what. He could only answer our questions with *yes* or *no*.

"I know this game," I said. "We call it Twenty Questions where I come from. Okay. Think of a hard one."

With a twinkle in his eye, just like Mrs. Figglehopper gets, Scrooge's nephew laughed, then nodded. "All right, I have one. Ask away!"

Frankie and I and the other guests asked a bunch of questions. It turned out the thing was an animal that lived in London, that grunted and growled but wasn't in a zoo and wasn't a horse, a cow, a bull, a tiger, a dog, a pig, a cat, or a bear.

At last, Scrooge's niece jumped up. "Oh, Fred, I know! It's your Uncle Scro-o-o-oge!"

"Yes, it is!" cried Fred, nearly falling on the floor.

I protested. "Hey, that's not fair. I was thrown off when you said it wasn't a bear!"

Scrooge scowled at me for an instant, then laughed.

Finally, Fred raised his glass. "A merry Christmas and a happy New Year to the old man—whatever he is!"

Scrooge himself seemed as jolly as I'd ever seen him, but soon, and despite his protests, the ghost waved his arm and whole scene passed away as if it were nothing but clouds.

After that, the ghost took us on a whirlwind tour of what seemed like the whole world of 1843. We visited hospitals and jails. We went to the front lines where troops were fighting in a distant war. We visited rich people and poor people, kids and old folks, in the country, and in cities. Every place was different, but they were all the same, too. Because wherever we went, we heard bells chiming and songs sung and people cheering "Merry Christmas!" to one another.

And all the while, the ghost grew older, clearly older.

With each new scene, the spirit's brown hair and beard were turning more and more gray, and his plump red cheeks were thinning and pale. He didn't seem so huge, either, but walked more slowly and hunched over.

"Oh, no," I whispered to Frankie, "Christmas is getting old. That must mean the holiday is ending."

Scrooge noticed it, too. "Spirit, tell me, are your lives so short?"

"My life on this earth is very brief," said the ghost. "It ends at midnight tonight. And my time is coming near."

In fact, it must have been the very end of the whole Christmas season. The street he brought us to was lonely and deserted. He walked slowly for a bit, then stopped and turned to us.

It was when he swished his robes around that I noticed something sticking out from beneath it. It wasn't his foot, though, and I couldn't help staring at it.

"What is that?" I asked.

"It looks like some kind of claw," said Frankie.

"It might be a claw," said the ghost. "Behold!"

He tugged his robe aside sharply, and there were two small children shivering on the ground at his feet. But they weren't cute little children like the ones you see in magazines and catalogs. They were all skinny and pale. Their eyes were sunken. They looked hungry, cold, and afraid.

Scrooge staggered back. "Spirit! Who are they? Are they . . . your children?"

"They belong to everyone," said the ghost, his jolly voice turning sharp and echoing in the deserted street. It sent chills up and down my spine to hear him now.

"And they cling to me—to Christmas—for help. This boy is Ignorance. He cannot learn, and the world fears him. This girl is Want. She is all the poor children in the world whom no one will take care of. Beware them both, but most of all beware this boy. If Ignorance takes over, there is no hope for any of us! Mark me—Ignorance means doom for everyone!"

"But have they no place to go?" asked Scrooge.

"Are there no prisons?" said the spirit, his voice booming now. "Are there no workhouses?"

I gasped. "Those are Scrooge's own words!"

"Are there no prisons?" thundered the ghost, his hair now white. "Are there no workhouses? Prisons! Workhouses! Prisons! Prisons!"

"No more!" said Scrooge. "I don't want to be haunted anymore. No more. No more!"

"Prisons! Workhouses!" boomed the ghost.

"I want to go home!" cried Scrooge. "Ghost, haunt me no more!" He jerked away from the spirit and accidentally knocked the book from Frankie's hands. It struck the street at the same time that a sharp wind barreled between the buildings. The wind took the book with it, tumbling end over end on the rough cobblestones, flipping the pages.

Kkkk! The sky crackled with sudden lightning.

"Meltdown!" cried Frankie. "Devin, get the book!"

Too late. Even as I ran after it, the wind whipped over the pages of the book wildly.

Suddenly there was an enormous ripping sound, as a big V of darkness pierced the sky.

Even as he called out "Prisons! Workhouses!" once more, the Ghost of Christmas Present vanished into the night air and the two ragged children with him.

"What is happening?" shouted Scrooge, losing his balance as the ground seemed to rush up at us.

"Story—going—haywire!" I shouted, finally reaching the book. "Got—it!"

I snapped it shut, but it had already gone to the next chapter. It was only a few pages, but it was enough to change everything.

The wind stopped howling, the lightning ceased. It was the same street, but the temperature had dropped by about a million degrees. The air was frigid.

And it had begun to snow heavily.

"Uh-oh," I said, shivering. "This is not good. Where's Scrooge's bedroom? We always go back to the bedroom to start a new ghost. I don't like this. Frankie, this is scary. Frankie—"

"Devin," she gasped suddenly, "remember what Jacob Marley said? The final ghost will come at midnight. Well, take a look—"

I squinted through the night to see the tower of a church. The hands on its clock were straight up.

Bong! The clock struck twelve times.

"Midnight," whispered Scrooge.

And as the last stroke of the clock ceased to ring, we lifted our eyes and saw it coming.

A solemn phantom, draped and hooded, coming, coming, coming, like a mist along the ground.

"N-n-now *that*," I whispered, "is what I c-c-call a g-g-ghost!"

Chapter 14

We all dropped to our knees as the phantom moved slowly and silently up the street to us.

This spirit wasn't in happy clothes like the last one. It was shrouded in a deep black cloak that hid its head, its face, its feet. Everything, in fact, except one thing.

A long, pale, bony, outstretched hand.

A hand I had seen twice before.

"Frankie, that's—"

"I know," she said.

"He keeps stealing my—"

"I know!"

"So ask for it back—"

"Are you out of your mind? Take a look at the guy!"

"Okay. But how about later?"

"Devin—shhhh!"

The spirit stopped over us. It said nothing.

Quivering, Scrooge raised his eyes to the hooded creature. "Are you the Ghost of Christmas Yet to Come?"

The spirit only pointed its bony hand forward.

"And will you show me shadows of things that have not yet happened, but *will* happen in the time to come?"

"And will you show me my backpack?" I asked.

Again, the spirit made no answer.

"Excuse me," I said, "but we're talking here. Are you going to answer us?"

The phantom was deadly silent under its hood.

"Not exactly a chatty sort of guy," I whispered.

The folds of the ghost's cloak trembled slightly as if it heard that and turned its head toward me for a second. As creepy as the spirit was, it was even creepier thinking that it was looking at me. I had goose pimples all over. Even my goose pimples had goose pimples!

"So you're not going to speak at all?" asked Frankie

The spirit only turned and pointed its awful hand into the dark streets ahead.

"We'll take that as a *no*," Frankie said.

"Ghost of the Future!" Scrooge cried. "I fear you more than any spirit I have seen! But as I know your purpose is to do me good, I follow you with a thankful heart. Lead on, Spirit, lead on!"

The phantom moved away, and we followed it. And even though we had been in a deserted section of London, bustling streets and big buildings suddenly surrounded us. Well-dressed men with top hats and long coats were chitchatting at each corner.

"These are men of business," said Scrooge, looking every which way. "I see them every morning before work. I know them."

The spirit stopped and pointed to one little group of men standing under a stone arch. We listened to them.

"No," said a great big chubby guy with several chins, "I don't know much about it. I only know he's dead."

"When did he die?" asked another.

"Last night, I believe," said the first.

A third man chuckled heartily. "I thought he'd never die! What has he done with his money?"

"He hasn't left it to me, that's all I know," said the man of many chins. "I'll go to the funeral, as long as there will be lunch. But unless I'm fed, I don't go!"

The others nodded and went their separate ways.

Scrooge looked at the spirit. "Why did we listen to

that? Were those men talking about someone I know?"

Without answering, the phantom glided on into another street. Its finger pointed to two men meeting outside a big stone bank.

"Maybe these guys will give us a clue," said Frankie.

"Yes, yes," said Scrooge. "I know them, too. They are wealthy men. They know me. Let's listen."

"How are you?" said one man.

"Good. And you?"

"Fine," said the first. "I hear he finally died."

"So I am told," said the second man. "Cold, isn't it?"

"Seasonable for Christmastime," said the first. "Do you like to ice-skate?"

"No, no. I can't afford to break anything! See you!"

"See you!"

The guys waved to each other and wandered off.

"That was it?" I said. "It didn't sound too important."

Scrooge blinked. "What was that about? Were they talking about Jacob Marley?"

"Probably not," I said. "This ghost is all about the future, and that happened way in the past." I turned to Frankie. "Maybe we should crack open the book again. It might give us a clue, because right now I'm feeling fairly clueless."

"Same old feeling, huh?" Frankie opened to the page we were on and immediately rubbed her eyes. "Whew, the words are pretty blurry, but it looks like we're heading into another part of London. A not nice part. I think things will get worse."

Scrooge frowned. "I never go to the bad parts of the city. Even so, it must all mean something. I shall especially observe the shadow of myself when it appears. What I say and do will be clues to sorting this out."

"Sounds like a plan," I said. "Okay, Spirit, next stop!"

Like the book said, we did move quickly into a part of London we hadn't seen before. The first thing that hit us was the smell. It was a cross between garbage and locker room mixed with sewers and old basements.

"Whew!" said Frankie, holding her nose. "Stinky!"

But that wasn't the worst part.

The whole place felt dangerous.

The streets were narrow and winding, the shops and houses were crooked and dark. The street beneath our feet sloshed with thick mud and puddles. The few people we did see were dressed in rags and kept to the shadows.

"What is this terrible place?" asked Scrooge.

"The nineteenth century at night," said Frankie.

The spirit moved along the street, passing before a low-roofed building, a sort of shop. A smear of yellow candlelight flickered from inside its greasy windows.

"Yuck," I said. "I'm glad we're not going in there."

Of course, we went in there. As if the walls were nothing, we passed into a room filled with rags, bottles, and giant piles of rusty metal keys, nails, chains, and broken hinges. You could hardly put your foot down without crunching on something. In the next room were chairs stacked one upon the other, most of them broken, piles of wood, shattered jars, and busted lamps.

"Uckh! This is so disgusting!" Frankie gasped.

"It's even worse than my bedroom," I muttered.

And there in the middle of it all, next to a charcoal stove made of blackened bricks, sat a man.

He was old and fat, with gray hair that hung down his face in ragged strands.

He tossed away a chicken bone, burped loudly, then picked up a pipe and blew out a smelly puff of smoke.

"Um, okay," said Frankie, still pinching her nose. "If I wasn't grossed out before, I am now!"

"Yeah," I added. "I feel Mrs. Cratchit's wonderful supper making another return visit—"

Just then, a woman with a heavy bundle crept

into the room, creaking across the floor right through us, which, if I needed to feel yuckier, sure did the trick.

Another woman, also with a bundle, followed her in.

The floors creaked a third time when a man in a faded black coat entered.

The fat man with the pipe jiggled as he sat, then burst into laughter. "Well, all three at once! What a surprise! Open the bundles, then. Let me see what you've brought me today. Come, come! What have you got?"

The first woman laughed. "Things a dead man won't miss. I say, if he wanted to keep them after he died, he'd have made more friends when he was alive—"

"A truer word was never spoken," said the second woman. "There he was, gasping out his last breath all alone. It's a judgment on him, I say. Open the bundles Joe, and tell us what you'll pay for them."

"Who is this poor dead man they speak of?" said Scrooge to the spirit. Of course, the spirit said nothing.

Out of courtesy, the guy in black went first. He produced a small bag. Old Joe plunged his greasy hands in and came out with some buttons, a handful of pins, and a watch on a chain.

"Not much," said Joe. He came up with a number, and paid the man out of a tin box. "Who's next?"

The second woman had a few bowls, some towels, two shiny spoons, and a couple of pairs of boots.

Old Joe looked them over, then cast his eyes to the cracked ceiling, closed them, and came out with a number. "Don't ask for more, or I'll lower my price!"

"Now undo my bundle, Joe," said the first woman.

Joe went down on his knees and untangled knot after knot, finally dragging out a large and heavy roll of dark cloth.

"What's all this then?" he asked. "Bed curtains?"

"Bed curtains!" the woman replied.

Joe coughed. "You don't mean to say that you took them down, rings and all, with him lying there dead?"

"I did! And look at this!" She held up a long nightgown. "They would have wasted it, if I hadn't taken it."

"What do you mean, wasted it?" asked Joe. "Do you mean you . . . er . . . took it off . . . er . . . his *body*?"

"I did!" she exclaimed.

The four of them had a creepy round of laughs at that.

I pulled Frankie and Scrooge back. "Okay, this is, like, the completely grossest thing ever. But I think I know what's going on. These people stole stuff from the dead guy, whoever he was, and they're selling it for money."

"Poor man!" said Scrooge. "Perhaps the spirit is showing me these things because I might end up like this poor dead fellow, whoever he is."

"Harsh lesson," I said. "Not quite as much fun as being at Fred's happy, clean, safe Christmas party—"

The people laughed again, and then all began to share Joe's pipe, quickly filling the room with blue smoke.

"Spirit, take me away from this dreadful place," said Scrooge, pinching his nose. "Show me some tenderness about a death. Yes, tenderness and love!"

With a wave of the ghost's dark cloak, old Joe and his guests were gone, and so were we.

Dark, cold mist rolled over us.

All of a sudden a soothing voice spoke out of the fog.

"'And he took a child and set him in the midst of them. . . .'"

It was a voice we knew.

Chapter 15

The words seemed to come from the darkness itself, but when the spirit lowered its robe, we found ourselves in a small room.

"We've been here before," said Frankie.

I knew it, too. It was the Cratchits' house. It was Christmastime, again, and there was snow falling outside the window. Only there was a difference.

As loud and bustling as it had been the first time we were there, now the house was quiet. Very quiet.

The noisy little Cratchits were now as still as statues in one corner. Mrs. Cratchit and her older daughters were sewing by the fire. They couldn't see us this time.

Behind us, Peter was sitting at a table with a

book in front of him. He was reading from it out loud.

"'And he took a child and set him in the midst of them,'" he repeated. Then he looked up to see his mother put down her sewing and put her hands to her face.

"The color hurts my eyes," she said. "And I wouldn't show your father weak eyes for anything. It must be time for him to come home."

"Past time," said Peter. "But I think he's walked a little slower than he used to."

They were very quiet again. At last, Mrs. Cratchit said, "I have known him walk with—I have known him walk with Tiny Tim on his shoulder very fast indeed."

"So have I," said Peter.

"And so have I," exclaimed one of the daughters.

"But he was so light to carry," the mother went on. "And his father loved him so, that it was no trouble, no trouble . . . ah, there is your father at the door!"

The door opened quietly behind us and Bob Cratchit stood there, alone. Mrs. Cratchit and the little ones brought him to the fireplace and sat him down.

"I wish you could have seen the place," he said at last. "It would have done you good to see how green a spot it is. But you'll see it often. I promised him that we would visit him every Sunday. And that we would never . . . we would never . . . forget him . . . oh! My little, little Tim! My Tiny Tim!"

He broke down all at once, and we did, too. Frankie began sobbing. In a flash, my cheeks were rolling with tears. Even Scrooge was shuddering and weeping.

It was the future, and Tiny Tim had died.

We stood for what seemed like forever watching the poor Cratchit family mourn for their little boy. I suddenly felt like those ghosts at the beginning who tried to help the poor woman on the street but couldn't.

"This stinks," I whispered, trying to dry my face. "I feel so helpless. Isn't there anything we can do?"

As usual, the ghost said nothing, which was really starting to get to me. It knew stuff. It just wouldn't tell us. All it did was turn and point its finger to the door.

"Spirit," said Scrooge, wiping his eyes, "something tells me that we must part soon. Show me what connection there is between Tiny Tim's death and the other scenes you have shown us. Show us who that dead man was—"

Without a word, the Ghost of Christmas Yet to Come raised its cloak, and a dark fog rolled over the Cratchit's living room, and the scene changed once more.

We stood before an iron gate.

On the other side was a graveyard.

"Sooner or later, there's always one of these," I said.

"Now we shall discover who those businessmen were speaking of," said Scrooge. "And whose possessions were being sold at that terrible shop. Yes, this will be good. I will try to avoid that poor man's fate. Oh, yes, I shall!"

The ghost moved among the gravestones, its long black cloak darker than the darkness of the yard. Over the weeds it walked until it stopped over one grave. Its hand moved slightly, and its finger pointed to the stone.

Scrooge staggered forward slowly. "Spirit, before I draw nearer to that stone, answer me one question. Are these the shadows of things that *must* be? Or are they shadows of things that *may* be?"

The ghost remained silent.

"I know that the way we lead our lives will lead to certain ends," said Scrooge. "But if we change our lives, the ends will change, too, won't they? Spirit, tell me it is not too late to change our lives. Tell me it's not too late!"

From the depths of the spirit's hood came no sound. It pointed only from the grave to Scrooge and back again.

"Fine, then," I said. "If you won't tell us, then we'll have to look for ourselves. Everyone together."

And so, together, Frankie, Scrooge, and I crept toward the cold gray stone.

Following the spirit's pale, bony finger, we read the name chiseled into the rough surface: EBENEZER SCROOGE.

Scrooge gave out a wail like Marley's ghost way back at the beginning of the book. "Ohhhhhh! No, no, no!"

The finger still pointed at Scrooge's gravestone.

"Spirit!" Scrooge screamed, clutching at its robe for the first time. "Hear me, now! I am not the man I was! I will not be the man under this stone! Why show me this, if I am past all hope? Why show me, if it's too late to change?"

For the first time, the ghostly hand appeared to shake.

"Good Spirit," Scrooge said, still clutching the robe and sinking to the ground, "I will honor Christmas in my heart, and try to keep it all year long! I will live in the past, the present, and the future. Yes, I will! The spirits of all three shall work within me. I will not shut out the lessons you have taught me! I will share everything I have! Oh, tell me that I may erase the writing on this stone! Do not let me die! I want to change!"

Scrooge grasped the bony hand. It tried to pull away, but Scrooge was like a young man in strength, holding on tight.

Frankie turned to me. "Everyone deserves a chance to change. Let's help Scrooge!"

I grinned. "Right on!"

We both leaped to Scrooge's aid, grabbing on to the spirit's icky hand. Strangely, it wasn't as cold as I thought it would be. But that wasn't the big surprise.

The big surprise was what fell out of the spirit's cloak the moment Frankie and I grabbed on.

It was purple.

And it smelled like chocolate chips.

I nearly choked when I saw it. "My backpack! It *was* you! You kept stealing it from me! Well, no more! I'm going to take it back! It's mine, and I need it—"

I grabbed the pack by the straps, but so did the phantom. No matter how I tried to pull it away, the cloaked spirit wouldn't let it go. Finally, I had an idea.

"Frankie—flip those pages!"

"Devin, I don't know. We'll go into major meltdown!"

"It's the only way to get the ghost out of this scene and us into the next one," I said, still tugging. "Frankie, I need those cookies to share with people. If Mr. Bony Hands takes them away, I'll never get the chance. I'll never be able to make it right. I'll be like those ghosts howling in the air, all helpless and weird!"

"Yes, Frankie," said Scrooge, his own skinny hands tugging at the pack. "Give Devin the chance to change!"

Frankie blinked. "I'm way not sure about this, but I'll do it. Only fasten your seat belts, people—we're in for a bumpy ride!"

As Scrooge and I tussled with the ghost, Frankie opened the little red book to where we were and flipped first one page, then another, and another.

Kkkk! The air crackled with sudden blue lightning.

A jagged black rip tore across the sky over us. It looked as if the sky were a giant page tearing in half right over our heads.

"I don't like this!" cried Frankie as a powerful dark wind began to howl. Thunder boomed all around us. Lightning bolts flashed everywhere.

Still the spirit wouldn't let go.

"You can't stop me!" I said. "I'll share my cookies! I will! There is no next time! I'll do it now! It's not too late. It's not too late!"

Scrooge pulled and tugged at the dreadful spirit, saying the same thing. "It's not too late! No, no! I'm not the man I was! I'm not the man I was—"

"I'm not the boy I was!" I yelled.

"And I'm not the girl!" said Frankie. "I'll share all the time, everything!"

She flipped one more page, and—*kkkkk!*—suddenly, the cloak and hood and hand shrank, collapsed, and dwindled down to nothing but a wooden bedpost.

A wooden bedpost . . .

And a chocolate-smelling backpack.

Chapter 16

And there we were, huddled on Scrooge's bed in his room at home.

"Hooray!" Frankie cheered, leaping up. "Old creepy Mr. Bony Hands is gone, and we're not. We're here!"

"And my backpack is here!" I shouted.

"And my bed is here," said Scrooge. "And my room is here, and I am here! Yes, yes, yes! And best of all, the time before me is my own—to make myself a better person!"

"Me, too!" I cried, giving my pack a great big hug.

"Me, three!" said Frankie, jumping from the bed and running to the window, where she threw open the shutters and let blazing sunlight flood into the room.

"It's morning," she said. "I can hardly believe it. No more dark and foggy midnights for us."

"Hooray!" I cheered.

Scrooge tried to get serious for a moment even though his mouth kept wanting to laugh. "You know, Frankie and Devin, I have decided to live in the past, present, and future, yes I have. And you should, too. And the spirits of all three shall live within me, yes they will. That is what I will do—do—do—ha—ha—ha!"

He tried to be serious, but it couldn't last. He bellowed out a great big hearty laugh. "Oh, Jacob Marley. Oh, heaven. Oh, Christmastime be praised. All my things are here. I am here!"

Suddenly, he was spinning on his heels and prancing around the room, touching everything. "Look there!" he chirped. "That's the door Jacob Marley came in, dragging all his heavy chains—"

"And there's the corner where the Ghost of Christmas Present sat," said Frankie, pointing to the fireplace.

"And here's the window where we saw the wandering ghosts," I said, running to it.

Together, we all peeked out to see a bright, snow-filled street. The poor woman and her baby who were huddling out there that first night were—of course—long gone. Then, suddenly, all the bells in London seemed to ring at once, and a young boy came tearing into the street, sliding up and down the icy sidewalk.

"Boy!" Scrooge called out. "What day is it today?"

"Today?" said the boy. "Why, it's Christmas Day!"

"What?" said Frankie, jumping up and down. "We haven't missed it? How incredibly awesome. I guess ghosts can do stuff like that."

"Stuff like that?" said Scrooge, surprised. "Well, yes. They can do anything, can't they? Of course they can!"

Scrooge then leaned out the window again. "Boy, go to the grocer's shop around the corner and bring back the grocer with the largest turkey in the shop. Come back in five minutes, and I'll give you half a crown—"

"Yes, sir!" called the boy, and he was off like a shot.

"Ho, ho. I'll send the turkey to Bob Cratchit's," said Scrooge, rubbing his hands as if he were hatching a devious scheme. "He won't know who sent it. Oh, my, but it's twice the size of Tiny Tim!"

With his shaking hands he wrote out the address label, and when the grocer came sent him right away to bring it to the Cratchit household.

"I don't know what to do," Scrooge cried suddenly, laughing in a way I never thought possible of him. "I am as light as a feather. I am as happy as an angel. I am as merry as a schoolboy! Ha, ha!"

"You should laugh more often," I told him.

"I should," said Scrooge. "I will!"

"Yeah, it's a great laugh," said Frankie. "It sounds like your nephew's laugh."

Scrooge wrinkled up his eyes. "My nephew? Oh, my. Yes, of course. We must go there. Right now. If he'll still have me."

Frankie smiled. "Something tells me he will. And I'm not just reading ahead, either."

"Then let's go spread some Christmas cheer," said Scrooge, his lips in a new and probably permanent grin. "Christmas? Christmas! Yes, I do like the sound of the word. Christmas! Christmas! Come on, everybody."

He dressed up in his finest suit, I slung my trusty pack over my shoulder, and we went out into the world.

It was a sparkling morning. People were bustling up and down the street, and Scrooge, no longer keeping his head down, looked everyone in the face, smiled, and wished them a merry Christmas.

It was amazing to see and hear!

We hadn't gone far when a chubby man wandered up the street toward us.

"Look, it's the one of the charity guys from your

office," said Frankie. "The ones who wanted money."

We both looked at Scrooge to see how he would react to the guy he had practically thrown out of his office.

Scrooge frowned first, then brightened. "Frankie, Devin," he said. "Watch this. Oh, sir? Sir—"

The man looked over at Scrooge, then stopped, his face going pale. He turned and started off the other way.

As if he were half his age, Scrooge dashed after the man and caught up with him. "Merry Christmas, sir!"

The guy's eyes bugged and his mouth dropped open.

Scrooge laughed. "Yes, well, I suppose you didn't think you'd see me again. But if you please, I would like to give . . ." He then whispered something to the man.

"Lord bless me, Mr. Scrooge," said the chubby man. "Are you serious, sir?"

"Oh, he's serious," I said. "He's changed."

"And not a penny less," said Scrooge. "Many back payments are included in that amount, I assure you."

"Then I thank you," said the man. "And the poor people of London thank you, too."

"Pish-posh! No thank-yous, please. It is my duty as a human being. Now, a merry Christmas to you, sir!"

And the man hustled off, probably to tell his partner the unbelievable story.

"That was so cool," said Frankie. "You really have changed."

"That was just the beginning," said Scrooge. "What good are my riches if I do not share them. They will be like, like—"

"Like cookies," I said, tapping my backpack. "It's like cookies that spoil if you keep them locked away and don't share them. And I need to share mine."

Scrooge looked at me. "Good idea. Wonderful idea, in fact. But first, let me share. Come and watch this!"

We followed Scrooge to church, where he dropped a stack of money in the collection plate. Then we walked through some more streets, with Scrooge digging into his pockets for any kid who sang a Christmas song.

Finally, we came to a brick house on a quiet lane. We marched to the door, Scrooge knocked, and it opened.

"Ha-ha! Ha-ha!" boomed a great familiar voice.

It was Scrooge's nephew Fred, a sudden smile beaming from his surprised face. "Why, Uncle Scrooge! You came! Frankie! Devin! Come in! Come right in!"

Scrooge sighed. "If your invitation is still open . . ."

"It is," said Fred. "Of course, it is! My dear, look who's here." Suddenly, his wife was behind him, her eyes twinkling and beaming with joy just like Fred's.

Naturally, there was a party. In fact, it was pretty much the same party Frankie and I had gone to with the Ghost of Christmas Present, except that Scrooge played the Yes and No game, and this time he wasn't the answer. I was! After that, someone shouted for music, and everyone began springing around the room.

Since dancing is pretty much at the top of my list of things to never do, I spent most of the time chowing at the overflowing munchie table.

It was there that I thought of something.

I turned to see Frankie huddled in a quiet corner with the book. "Can I read, too?" I asked. "I need to find out something."

Frankie looked up. "Have a seat."

So we shared the last few pages of the book together. It was then and there that I got my idea.

Soon enough, we were back in Scrooge's office. It was the next morning, December 26, the day after Christmas. Scrooge had come in early, and there he was sitting behind his big old black desk, waiting for Bob and practically giggling his head off.

"Oh, what a surprise," he said with a laugh. "Bob

will be astonished. The look on his face will be price-less!"

"What surprise?" I asked.

Scrooge winked. "Just you wait. This will be sooooo good. Now hide. Hide!"

We crouched behind Scrooge's desk, out of sight.

The clock struck nine. No Bob Cratchit came into the office. A quarter past nine. No Bob.

"Uh-oh, he's late," whispered Frankie.

"Even better!" said Scrooge. "Even better!"

At eighteen and a half minutes after nine, the door opened and Bob slid in. He quickly and quietly wound his two scarves on the coatrack and slipped onto his stool.

Scrooge, sounding very much like his old self, growled like a grizzly bear. "Bob Cratchit! What do you mean by coming in here at this time of day?"

We peeked over the top of the desk.

"I'm very sorry, sir," said Bob, stepping slowly into Scrooge's office. "I am a bit late, sir—"

"You are!" snarled the old guy. "And I am not going to stand for this sort of thing any longer! Therefore—"

Scrooge leaped from his desk and poked Bob in the shoulder with his finger. "Therefore, I am going to—*raise your salary!*"

For an instant, it looked as if Bob was going to turn and run for his life, or at least find something to defend himself with. He even eyed the ruler on Scrooge's desk.

Then Frankie and I jumped up. "Surprise, surprise! Scrooge is nice now!"

Bob staggered on his feet. "What . . . what . . ."

Scrooge dug him again in the shoulder, and burst out in cheery laughter. "A merry Christmas, Bob!"

Bob blinked. "A merry . . . what?"

"Yes! Yes! A merry Christmas, Bob! A merrier Christmas, than I have ever given you before! Yes! I will raise your salary, and try to help you raise that wonderful, wonderful family of yours—if you will let me. Yes! Yes, Bob! And we will discuss all this today, over a bowl of steaming Christmas punch! What do you think of that?"

What Bob thought of it was hard to tell. He stared at Scrooge as if one of them had gone completely wacko.

"Bob," said Scrooge, who seemed to like saying his name, "Bob, I am a changed man now. I am different. And I want to help you all I can. So! Now! You run out and get more coal for your fire. Yes, and you do that, before you dot another *i*, Bob Cratchit!"

Finally, Bob broke into a smile. He gave out a happy yelp and hustled right out of the room, to the merry peals of Scrooge laughing and singing Christmas carols.

Frankie and I joined in the singing, too.

Then it happened.

When Bob sprang out through the front door, light flooded into Scrooge's office from the street.

But it wasn't regular London light from 1843.

It was a flickery blue light.

And it was coming from a couple of things that weren't around a hundred and a half years ago.

I gasped to see them. Frankie did, too.

"The zapper gates!"

Chapter 17

While Scrooge laughed and laughed, Frankie and I stepped out of the office and over to the gates. Their blue sparks sizzled in the crisp, cold Christmas-y air.

"Is it time already?" I said. "I mean, there's still stuff to do, isn't there?"

Frankie opened the book. There was only one page left. "Scrooge is changed. Everything is good. The zapper gates are here. Don't you want to go back home?"

"I do," I said. "Sort of. But I also . . . I want to go back two days."

"Devin—"

"Frankie, I mean it. It's been bothering me since

126

Marley's ghost opened that window and we looked out. You know what I mean."

"I know what you mean, but what about the zapper gates?" she said. "What if they fade?"

"We just have to hope they don't," I said. "I have to take care of this. Look, it's okay. You can stay here and listen to Scrooge laugh, but I won't be able to laugh—not really—until I do this one last thing."

Frankie cracked a grin. "Yeah, right. After all we've been through? As if I'm going to let you go bouncing around a classic book all by yourself."

I knew what she really meant to say. It felt good to hear it. "Frankie. You know, I really do—"

"Say it, and I'll whack that troublemaking backpack right over your weird head."

I laughed. "Okay, okay. Then, come on. We'll be back before the gates fade. I promise."

"Don't promise," she said. "Just hope."

I opened the book to the exact page we were on. Then I did something I'd never done before.

I did a reverse flip. Back through the book.

All the way back to page 51.

"Brace yourself, Frankie," I said. "It's meltdown time!"

I expected the nice bright Christmas sky to turn black and me and Frankie to get tumbled like T-shirts in a dryer. But it didn't, and we didn't. Instead, a calm, warm breeze fluttered out of the fluttering pages of the book.

"Whoa. This is unexpected!" I said.

Frankie grinned suddenly. "And I bet I know why. It's okay to go back and reread parts of a book. In fact, books are made for rereading!"

"That is so cool!" I said. "I'm telling you, if you try, you can learn something new just about every day."

When the pages stopped fluttering, the warm breeze stopped, too, and the bright sky faded, and there we were, out on the dark street outside Scrooge's house.

It was Christmas Eve again. Icy wind was moaning between the buildings. Snow was falling. And the air was filled with the howling of phantoms, all rushing around, throwing their arms up, pleading and howling.

"It's just like it was when we were here before," I said.

"I didn't like it much the first time," said Frankie.

"But this will be different," I said. "I promise."

Looking up, we saw Marley's ghost float out Scrooge's window and join the spirits howling in the air. "There," said Frankie, pointing through the thickening snow. "I know that's why you came. There she is."

And there she was, that poor woman huddled on a doorstep of the building across Scrooge's street.

She tried to keep her baby covered against the falling snow, but it was coming down very heavily now.

The spirits around us wailed and moaned.

"The ghosts are trying to help her," said Frankie. "But they can't. It's too late for them."

"But not for us," I said. "I think that's the real lesson of this book. That maybe you can have a second chance, if you really want one. Come on, Frankie."

We made our way over to the woman. She seemed startled and afraid to see us. She held her baby closer.

"Hey," I said. "I just wanted to give you something."

I unslung my pack, pulled open the top, and took out the plastic container of cookies. I popped open the lid and the air blossomed with the smell of chocolate chips.

Those cookies smelled so good. I could eat every one of them right then and there. But I didn't want to.

"Here," I said to the woman. "They're yours."

Her eyes grew large. "For me?"

"For you," I said. "It's not a lot, but maybe it'll help."

"And I have something, too," said Frankie. She dug into her pocket and pulled out the coin we got. "I don't know my old English coins, but maybe it's worth a little, at least."

The woman started to cry.

"No, no, don't do that," I said. "Your tears will freeze! Besides, it's Christmas Eve. Try to be happy. And as soon as you can, go and see Mr. Scrooge. I'm sure he'll help you. And your baby. I know he wants to."

At just that moment, the spirits seemed to fade into the mist and fog around us. Their voices faded together, too, leaving only the faint pealing of church bells.

The woman smiled at us, then bundled her baby up and made her way down the street, even as the snow stopped, and the sky began to grow brighter.

I gave a sigh. "Nice one, Frankie. I'd forgotten that coin. I can't imagine a better thing to do with it."

"Or a better way to use those cookies," she said. "Of course, now you'll be in trouble with Mr. Wexler, just like I am."

I chuckled at that. "Frankie, I can't imagine a better person to be in trouble with. Besides, do you think we could ever actually be *out* of trouble?"

She laughed. "I sort of hope not. It's too much fun. So, Devin, are we good to go?"

I closed up my backpack. "We're good to go."

Carefully, we moved ahead through the pages, seeing the story again in fast motion, until we were once again at Scrooge's office. I swear, even after our little detour back through the book, the guy was still at his desk, laughing like a crackpot.

"Good-bye, Mr. Scrooge," said Frankie. "It's been nice being haunted with you."

"Oh, we have had quite a time, haven't we?" he said, his cheeks all rosy. "I have learned so much during our travels. I've learned that it's wrong to cut myself off from everyone. And that the real joys of life are those you find with other people, with friends, and family. And that—while you have the power— you must help people, because *they* are what matter!"

"I should write that down for class," I whispered. "It sounds just like the theme of the book!"

Frankie grinned. "And it sounds like you got the Christmas spirit, all right, Mr. Scrooge. I'm sure Charles Dickens would be very happy."

"Who?" said Scrooge, laughing louder than ever. "Dear, dear, there are so many people I must meet. Yes, my two friends, I shall never forget our time together."

I knew for certain he never would.

"I'm glad you found your backpack," he said. "What was in it that you needed so badly?"

I thought about that. "I didn't really need it so badly, after all. But someone else did. So I gave it away."

Scrooge's eyes twinkled like an elf. "Then I wasn't

the only one who was helped by the spirits?"

"Nope," said Frankie. "I think we all were. And, by the way, a lady and a baby will probably come to see you today. Maybe you can—"

"I shall help them," he said. "It will be an honor."

"And now—" I held up the last page of the book. "I think it's time for us to go, and for you to get on with your life."

"Then let me wish you well," said Scrooge. "And to quote our friend Tiny Tim, 'God bless us, every one!'"

With that, we said our good-byes, dashed out of Scrooge's office, and sprang straight between the waiting zapper gates.

Kkkkk!

The whole old world of London in 1843 seemed to flash bright blue. Then everything went dark for a half second until—*blam!*—"Ouch!"—"Oof!"—Frankie and I slammed into the wall of the library workroom, the blue light vanished, and we were home.

At instant later, Mrs. Figglehopper stepped into the room. She blinked and shook her head.

"Why are you on the floor?" she asked, a slight smile starting on her lips. "Shouldn't you two be at the Christmas Banquet?"

Frankie jumped up. "We didn't miss it? Awesome!"

"You haven't been here *that* long," said Mrs.

Figglehopper. "Now, if you are quite done fixing that book, Mr. Wexler has asked that everyone join him in the cafeteria. The Christmas Banquet is about to begin."

"I want to help!" I said.

"Me, too!" said Frankie. "There's a lot we can do."

"That sounds like the Christmas spirit," Mrs. Figglehopper said.

I smiled. "Yeah, there's a lot of that going around."

Her eyes twinkled merrily, and she swished out the door and down the hall, singing, "Come! Come!"

When we entered the cafeteria, there was a line of people from Palmdale who needed food. Some of them weren't dressed very well, and there were kids there, which broke my heart. But it felt better when Frankie and I hopped into the serving line and got right to work.

While Mrs. Figglehopper sliced turkey, and Mr. Wexler put it on the plates, I gave everyone heaps of mashed potatoes and gobs of stuffing. Next to me, Frankie spooned out lakes of gravy and mounds of cranberries.

It was work, but it made me realize how much stuff I have, and I felt good doing a little bit to help people who didn't have as much. I had to thank the book for that. I could tell that Frankie felt the same way.

"Merry Christmas," we said to everyone who passed through the line.

Then, when things slowed down a bit, Mr. Wexler pointed to a podium set up with a microphone at one end of the cafeteria. "Would you care to read to us?" he asked. "A Christmas story would be nice."

Frankie and I looked at each other and grinned.

"I think we know the perfect story," said Frankie.

We hustled to the podium, and while everyone settled into their dinners, Frankie opened to the first page of the book, moving it over so both of us could read it.

"You start," she said, so I did, with the very first line.

"'Marley was dead: to begin with. There is no doubt whatever about that. . . .'"

For the next two hours, Frankie and I took turns reading while people came and went and ate and drank.

Finally, we got to the last page.

"'Scrooge was better than his word. He did it all and infinitely more. And to Tiny Tim, who did *not* die, he was a second father.'"

Then Frankie took over. "'He became as good a friend, as good a master, and as good a man as the good old city knew, or any other good old city, town, or borough, in the good old world.'"

"Lots of *good-old*s there," I said. "Should we keep going?"

"Please," said Mrs. Figglehopper. Mr. Wexler nodded.

"'And it was always said of him, that he knew how to keep Christmas well, if any man alive possessed the knowledge. May that truly be said of us, and all of us! And so, as Tiny Tim observed, God bless us, every one!'"

Everybody stood and cheered as we closed the book and headed to the tables for our own Christmas supper.

Plopping down into our seats, I said, "You know, Frankie, this is shaping up to be one of our best Christmases ever. Not bad for a couple of slackers, is it?"

"You said it," she said. "And I have to admit, Dev, I like happy endings. I like the way that Christmas can sort of, you know, make you a better person."

I thought about that, then grinned. "Just like books!"

"You can say that again!" chirped Mrs. Figglehopper, who had overheard us.

But we couldn't.

Our mouths were way too crammed with food.

135

Dear Reader:

Charles Dickens is one of my favorite authors, and I'm tickled pink that Devin and Frankie like him, too. Certainly, they seem to know A Christmas Carol backward and forward!

Even today, many readers call Dickens the greatest English novelist who ever lived. Certainly he was something of a superstar in his own day!

Born in Portsmouth, England, in 1812, Dickens remembered his early childhood as his happiest time. He loved to learn, liked school, and had an unquenchable passion for books (I can certainly appreciate that!).

When his family moved to London in 1822, things began to change. Dickens's father was sentenced to several months in a debtor's prison for not paying his bills. To make ends meet, Dickens was sent to work in a dismal factory pasting labels on bottles of boot polish. This experience affected him deeply. He became determined to make his fortune and never be poor again.

While still in his teens, Dickens started writing political and social news for London newspapers. Adopting the pen name Boz, he collected his writings in his first book, Sketches by Boz, and achieved some success.

But nothing prepared Dickens for the instant fame he would gain by writing the comical adventure novel The Pickwick Papers, when he was only twenty-four. Like nearly all of Dickens's later novels, Papers was first published in monthly installments. Tens of thousands of eager readers clamored for each new installment as quickly as he could write them. His fortune was made!

In quick sequence, Dickens wrote *Oliver Twist*, *Nicholas Nickleby*, and *The Old Curiosity Shop*, and, as if it were possible, became even more famous.

But Dickens never forgot his early hardships. In 1843 he hit on the idea of writing a Christmas book, but one that would have as a theme the plight of the poor and the importance of giving.

A Christmas Carol was born!

This delightful "ghost story of Christmas" remains one of Dickens's most famous and well-known works.

After writing the autobiographical *David Copperfield* (1850), and what many call his masterpiece, *Bleak House* (1853), Dickens embarked on a series of very popular but exhausting speaking tours throughout England and the United States. The strain of these tours weakened him. In 1870, he died at the age of fifty-eight, leaving his final work, *The Mystery of Edwin Drood*, unfinished.

To this day, Charles Dickens is universally beloved as a great writer, a witty and sensitive man, and a champion of the poor. Despite the 800-page length of some of his novels (yes, I can hear Frankie and Devin gasp!), he is read and enjoyed by every age, from children on up.

Try checking out his books—you'll make your librarian happy!

I. M. Figglehopper